Martha in the Mirror

Recent titles in the Doctor Who *series:*

FOREVER AUTUMN
Mark Morris

SICK BUILDING
Paul Magrs

WETWORLD
Mark Michalowski

WISHING WELL
Trevor Baxendale

THE PIRATE LOOP
Simon Guerrier

PEACEMAKER
James Swallow

SNOWGLOBE 7
Mike Tucker

THE MANY HANDS
Dale Smith

Martha in the Mirror

JUSTIN RICHARDS

2 4 6 8 10 9 7 5 3 1

Published in 2008 by BBC Books, an imprint of Ebury Publishing.
Ebury Publishing is a division of the Random House Group Ltd.

Doctor Who is a BBC Wales production for BBC One
Executive Producers: Russell T Davies and Julie Gardner
Series Producer: Phil Collinson

The Random House Group Ltd Reg. No. 954009.
Addresses for companies within the Random House Group can be found at www.randomhouse.co.uk.

A CIP catalogue record for this book is available from the British Library.

ISBN 978 1 84607 420 2

The Random House Group Limited supports the Forest Stewardship Council (FSC), the leading international forest certification organisation. All our titles that are printed on Greenpeace approved FSC certified paper carry the FSC logo. Our paper procurement policy can be found at www.rbooks.co.uk/environment

Series Consultant: Justin Richards
Editor: Stephen Cole
Project Editor: Steve Tribe
Cover design by Lee Binding © BBC 2008

Typeset in Albertina and Deviant Strain
Printed and bound in Germany by GGP Media GmbH, Poessneck

For Chris – my naughty twin…

I am the Man in the Mirror.

The castle was haunted by a young girl.

She was small and blonde, and maybe twelve years old. She was called Janna, and she wasn't a ghost – just a girl left to fend for herself, scavenging and begging and living off the goodwill of others. A shadow glimpsed in the kitchens, a flicker of movement in a corridor, a shape watching from an alcove. Like a ghost.

And Janna, in her turn, was also haunted. By her dead sister.

For a hundred years I have watched events unfold, fortunes rise and fall, lives saved and lost. I have laughed and I have wept. But I have never sought to return to the world of flesh and blood.

Until now.

It started the day the man looked in the mirror.

Janna wondered what was in the crate. She watched Bill and Bott carry it from the main gates across the courtyard. She ran along the battlements, keeping them in sight. Then down the winding stairs of Kaiser's Tower in time to hear Bill complaining about his latest software patch and Bott telling him to shut up and put his mechanical back into it.

They took the crate to the Great Hall. Janna crept after them, hiding in her favourite spot under a long side table. The faded velvet cloth hung down low and she lay full-stretch, elbows on the stone floor, chin in her cupped hands as she watched.

The crate contained a mirror, which was taller than Bill and wider than Bott. They struggled to lift it up and fix it to the wall. The bottom of the mirror was only just off the floor, and the top of it was higher than the cracked wood panel that Janna could touch if she jumped and stretched.

Bill and Bott stood in front of the mirror and looked at themselves. Bill wiped it over with a cloth. Bott inspected the ornate gilt frame.

'Nice workmanship, Bill,' Bott said.

'You're not wrong, Bott,' Bill agreed. 'You'd think it was really old.'

The mirror looked old to Janna.

'The real one would be,' Bott was saying.

'Well, obviously,' Bill agreed. 'Better tell His Nibs it's here then.'

'Oil break first,' Bott said. 'My joints are seizing up after that. It weighs a tonne.'

'Obviously oil break first,' Bill replied as he turned with a whirr of his mechanism and marched from the Great Hall. 'And you think your joints are playing *you* up...' he was saying as his voice faded away.

Janna was about to crawl out from under the table, about to skip across the room and have a proper look at the mirror that seemed old but wasn't. But someone else came into the hall, and she eased back to be sure she was out of sight.

The man stood in front of the mirror, just where Bill had been standing a few moments before. He stared into it, nodding as if pleased. His reflection nodded back, smiling.

He inspected the frame, tapped at the glass surface. From where she was lying, Janna could see that his expression – his real expression – was slowly changing from a smile to a frown.

'That can't be right,' the man murmured, just loud enough for Janna to hear.

But she wasn't listening. She was watching his face, his real face, as the frown deepened.

The man stood with his hands behind his back and stared at himself. His reflection stared back. The man tilted his head slightly, and so did the reflection. He took a step towards the mirror. The reflection stepped towards him. They regarded each other through a thin barrier of glass. Then the man brought his hands from behind his back to clasp them in front of him. He sighed.

The man raised a hand – frowning, curious, reaching out towards the mirrored surface. The reflection raised his hand too. Only the man in the mirror was smiling. And he was holding a gun.

The man – the real man – took a startled step backwards.

The sound of the shot echoed round the hall. Janna clasped her hand over her mouth and pulled back into the darkness beneath the table.

The glass bullet shattered its way into the man's heart. His body fell to the floor. His face was turned towards Janna, his eyes wide – staring at her lifelessly. And above and behind, Janna could see the man in the mirror – watching, and smiling, as he stepped through and into the room.

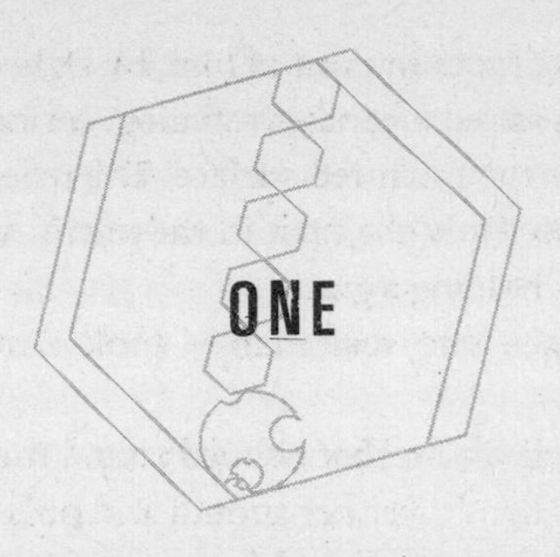

ONE

Her dead sister was following her. Janna could hear her feet on the stone floor of the corridor. She caught glimpses of her shadow on the wall, distorted by the flickering torchlight. She heard the girl whispering the name: 'Janna, Janna, Janna…'

Nowhere was safe. Her sister knew all the places, all the hidey-holes and the darkest shadows.

'All right,' she shouted into the gloom at the end of the passageway. 'It should have been me that died. I know that. I'm sorry. I can't change it – if I could, I would.' She sank to her knees. 'I'm so sorry. So sorry.'

The lights flickered impossibly as a breeze ruffled Janna's hair. The torches looked like real flame but they were run by the same fusion generators that powered everything in the castle. They wouldn't suffer in a breeze.

Still kneeling, Janna looked round. How could there be a breeze, here, deep under the castle? It was getting stronger, blowing her hair round her pale, grubby face. An unholy noise echoed off the stonework, growing and fading with the breeze – a rasping grating sound. The walls and floor were bathed with a blue light. Shadows in the nearest alcove deepened as the noise grew.

'Stop it,' Janna yelled into the fury. 'Stop this. I'm sorry!'

And it did stop. The wind died, the light faded, the noise was gone.

In its place a large blue box stood solid and confident in the alcove. Janna backed into the shadows and watched as a door in the front of the box opened and a man stepped out.

He was tall and thin with spiky hair and eyes that were wide with interest and amusement. Eyes that fixed unerringly on Janna despite the dark shadows that enfolded her.

'Hello,' the man said cheerfully. 'What's your name, then?' He took a step towards her, allowing the silhouette of a woman to step out of the box behind him, her face hidden behind the man's shoulder.

But Janna didn't wait to see the woman's face. She turned and ran. She could hear her sister's ghost running after her.

'It doesn't look like the most brilliant theme park in this part of the cosmos,' Martha said. 'It looks like a damp, gloomy tunnel.' She sniffed. 'And it smells.'

'It's not damp,' the Doctor said. He plunged his hands into his coat pocket and sniffed as well. 'Well, not really. Not *damp* damp. Doesn't smell too bad, either.' He peered into semi-darkness. 'I'll give you gloomy, though. Lots of gloom. Looming gloom. A real gloom loom, assuming gloom can loom.'

'So where are we really?'

'Really? Outside the TARDIS. In a smelly, gloomy, not-really-damp-damp tunnel, I should think. Pity that girl ran off, we could have asked her.'

'What girl?'

'The one that ran off. When she saw you.'

Martha's eyes widened. 'Excuse me, but it was you that frightened her off. I didn't even see her.'

The Doctor wasn't listening. He pulled the TARDIS door closed, then marched off down the gloomy passageway. 'Maybe we're a bit early,' he said. 'Maybe they just haven't opened yet.'

He hesitated as he reached a junction, pointing first one way then the other. 'Eeny meeny miny mo,' he murmured. He set off along the left-hand passageway. His delighted voice echoed back to Martha. 'Oh, it's mo!'

'Early as in, they're still having breakfast?' Martha wondered, catching him up.

'Or early as in the place is still a frontier fort under almost constant siege from either Anthium or Zerugma, and they haven't actually sorted out the peace treaty and built it yet.'

Martha ran to catch him up. 'You said guided tours and coffee shops,' she accused. 'Not frontier fort and constant siege. You said exhibitions and historical re-enactments.'

'Yeah,' the Doctor conceded. 'But so much better when you arrive in the middle of the real thing. I mean, just think about it.'

'I am thinking about it.'

'Real siege warfare. Real people in real situations. Real history.'

'Real blood, real death, real destruction and real danger.'

The Doctor paused to inspect one of the torches flickering on the wall. He seemed to be rolling the idea round his mouth. 'That too,' he decided eventually. 'You know, this isn't real though. Look at it – that's clever.'

Before Martha could stop him, he stuck his hand into the flames. 'It's all right,' he said, seeing her expression. 'Like I said. Not real. Brilliant, clever, real-*istic*. But not real. They must have a fusion generator somewhere. Means we can't be far off. War's probably been over for years.'

'Probably?'

He was off again. 'Well, possibly. Maybe.' He spun round and continued walking backwards so he could look at Martha behind him. 'I don't know – let's find out. We need to find someone to ask really. Like that little girl.'

Martha stopped.

The Doctor stopped too. 'What?' he asked, not turning to see what she was looking at.

'Maybe,' Martha said slowly, 'we could ask a sinister cloaked figure who looks like he's enrolled as Chief Frightener at the Monastery of Doom?'

The Doctor's eyes narrowed. 'Behind me?' he whispered, pointing over his own shoulder without looking.

Martha nodded.

'Sinister monk? Easy!' He spun round again. 'Hello brother, can you spare a... No, hang on, that's not it. I wonder if you can help us? Yes – that's right. Help – any chance?'

The monk was standing several metres further along the passageway. His head was slightly bowed so only darkness was visible under the hood of his black cloak. His hands were clasped in front of him, each folded into the opposite sleeve. As the Doctor spoke, the monk raised his head slightly. He lifted one hand – a pale, gnarled claw – and silently beckoned.

'Guided tour, you see?' The Doctor was off after the monk. 'Come on, Martha. Told you – historical re-enactment.'

'Yeah, but re-enacting what – the Black Death?'

'Could be. What did you expect?' the Doctor said as they followed the cloaked figure. 'The Spanish Inquisition?'

The monk led the Doctor and Martha up a flight of

twisting stone stairs into a wider, better-lit corridor. There were paintings on the walls and the slight smell of damp and decay faded.

They passed several other people – another monk, a soldier in armour that was clearly plastic, as if part of a child's dressing-up set, and a crocodile man. For a moment, when he first stepped out of a doorway, Martha thought he really was a crocodile man – scaly skin covered by strips of dark leather; clawed, reptilian feet and hands to match; a jutting snout that was full of teeth. Small dark eyes gleamed in the flickering light. Nostrils at the end of the snout seemed about to flare.

But then, they didn't. They sort of squashed inwards. And now Martha could see that the teeth were obviously painted on the mask. The claws on the feet bent like rubber as they caught on the paved floor. The reptilian skin was drawn onto the costume, not even moulded. Up close, it all looked a bit cheap. The gleaming eyes were staring through holes cut out of the mask.

The crocodile man raised his hand in greeting, and nodded. The mask shifted and looked in danger of falling off. Martha heard a sigh of irritation from inside. She smiled and waved back.

'What is this – fancy dress weekend?' Martha hissed at the Doctor.

'That was a Zerugian,' the Doctor said, apparently impressed.

'It was a costume. It was a man dressed up.'

'In full ceremonial battle armour.'

'In a cheap mask.'

They had stopped, and the monk was beckoning impatiently again. Martha frowned as she watched the withered hand with its talon finger curling. She reached out and grabbed the hand. It was squishy and the long nail on the end was bendy like the crocodile man's claws. It came off – a glove. Embarrassed now, Martha held it out for the monk to take back.

Under the hood, in the better light, Martha could see a young man – a very ordinary young man – staring back at her in surprise.

'Who are you? Where are we going?' Martha demanded.

The man shook his head slightly and put his finger to his lips as he pulled his glove back on.

'Silent order,' the Doctor said.

'He isn't even a real monk,' Martha said as they continued on their way.

'I didn't mean he *belongs* to a silent order of monks. I meant, he's been ordered to be silent.'

'But – why?'

'Been to Disneyland?' the Doctor asked.

'What's Disneyland got to do with it?'

'Does Mickey Mouse speak?'

'Sort of squeaks.'

The Doctor didn't reply, but followed the 'monk' through a doorway into a huge and impressive room. 'Now this is more like it. Thanks, Friar Tuck,' he said to the monk. 'Mickey Monk – what a nasty thought,' he murmured as the monk bowed and left. 'And you'd never get a hood to fit over the ears.'

Martha hardly noticed. She was looking round the room. It was enormous, like the banqueting hall of a huge medieval castle. A long table ran down the middle of the room, with other smaller tables off to each side. All were covered with the same faded, thinning velvet material. There were several figures in alcoves – knights in advanced armour like the costume she'd seen earlier, but more robust and made of heavy, dull metal – the real thing.

Paintings, darkened with age, hung on the walls. The far end of the great room was dominated by an ornate mirror that reached up from just above the floor to well above Martha's head. Two large futuristic guns, like rifles with battery packs added, were fixed in a cross over a round shield.

'Parallax rifles,' the Doctor said, seeing where Martha was looking. 'Nasty. They wobble your insides into a different place from your outsides. Then back again, which at least stops it getting messy. But the trauma's enough to kill even a Zerugian.'

'And where are we, exactly?'

'In Extremis. Which is where we're supposed to be. Judging by the pictures at least.' The Doctor was walking slowly round the room examining the paintings. 'Various battles between the Anthiums and Zerugians. Think I got the timing slightly wrong, but this is definitely Castle Extremis.'

'Greatest theme park in the cosmos?'

'Yeah. Well, it will be. One day. Looks like we've arrived before it really got going. In the years before the peace treaty it was all a bit cheap and cheerful. Well, cheap and dreadful, actually. Fusion generators, advanced battle fleets, and cheap plastic dressing-up costumes.'

There was a man standing in the doorway. Martha could see him reflected in the mirror, and she turned abruptly. The man was of slight build and wearing a plain, dark suit like Martha might expect to find in a department store. His dark hair was greying slightly at the temples and thinning slightly on top. But his craggy, lined face revealed he was older than his hair suggested.

'Can I help you?' the man asked in a rich, deep voice.

'Oh I do hope so,' the Doctor said. 'I'm sorry to turn up unannounced.'

'You are here for the...' the man's voice trailed off.

'The *thing*, yes. Don't tell me we're not on the list. Got my invite – complete with "plus one" on it and everything.' The Doctor was brandishing his wallet with the psychic paper.

'How come no one else will talk to us?' Martha asked as the man examined the paper – which would show him something relevant that he expected to see.

'Oh, a stupid rule. I suggested they do away with it for the duration of these sessions. I suggested they do away with the guides completely, come to that. But, well – tradition. That poor lad Gonfer had to write me a note saying you were here. The guides are not permitted to speak while in costume and on duty.'

'Mickey Mouse,' the Doctor said.

'The Doctor and Miss Mouse,' the man replied, nodding with interest. 'Welcome to Castle Extremis. It is an honour to have observers from the Galactic Alliance attend the Treaty Talks.'

'It's Martha, actually,' Martha explained. 'Just ignore him.'

'My apologies, Miss Martha Mouse.'

Martha glared at the Doctor.

'But it is so unusual for GA observers to declare themselves,' the man went on. 'I knew, of course, that two observers were in attendance, monitoring the proceedings. But in the normal run of things they remain anonymous, sending their reports surreptitiously and only intervening to use their very special powers of jurisdiction and release of weapons in extreme emergencies.'

'Well,' the Doctor said, 'unusual circumstances and all that. And you are?'

The man actually took a step backwards in surprise. His voice rose an octave either in shock or anger: 'I am High Minister Defron. I am the man who brought the two sides to the negotiating table in the first place and brokered the peace.'

The Doctor grinned and clapped High Minister Defron on the shoulder. 'Course you are,' he said. 'We knew that. Didn't we know that, Martha Mouse?'

'Yeah, like we know each other's names,' Martha said.

'Isn't that right, Doctor Donald Duck?'

'So,' the Doctor said as Defron led them along yet another corridor, 'why don't you fill us in on the way?'

The High Minister had told them he was taking them back to the negotiating chamber where they could meet the delegates from Anthium and Zerugma. 'Fill you in?' he asked, confused.

'The treaty conference,' Martha prompted. 'How did you manage it?'

'It's a big deal,' the Doctor said. 'Must have taken some doing. We'd like to know how you see the situation. From your perspective.'

'The press is not invited until we're ready for the final signing ceremony,' Defron said. 'This isn't a time for self-congratulation or for soundbites.'

'Course not.'

'Though I confess I feel the hand of history on my shoulder. What do you need to know?'

The Doctor's eyes widened, and he shot Martha a 'get him' look.

'The Doctor's the expert,' Martha said. 'Maybe you can give me the background. I'm kind of new to the team.'

'But a tremendous asset,' the Doctor assured her. 'Duck and Mouse – what a partnership. So whose idea was it to have the signing ceremony here at Castle Extremis?'

'It seemed the obvious place,' Defron said. 'There

may have been peace for twenty years, but Anthium and Zerugma are still technically at war.'

'Until the treaty is signed, right?' Martha said.

'If it is signed,' the Doctor said quietly.

'Oh it will be signed,' Defron assured them. 'We are down to the fine details now.'

They passed an open door. Through it Martha could see a room in the middle of being decorated. More than that; it was being renovated, she realised. An ornate fireplace was in pieces on the floor, and several of the firebrand wall lights had been pulled away, trailing wires.

'Be good when it's finished,' she said.

Defron shook his head. 'I despair of those two maintenance robots sometimes,' he said heavily. 'Just so long as the state rooms are ready in time. The rest can wait. They've managed with it in this condition for long enough, as a tourist attraction. Not that it was terribly popular, that's why they needed all those Lottery grants. Even so – who wants run-down facilities and gimmicky guides? The Galactic Alliance plan to turn the place into some sort of historical theme park after the treaty. A place the peoples of the cosmos can visit, where they can sigh at the mistakes of Anthium and Zerugma, and learn from their reconciliation.' He shook his head sadly.

'It'll never catch on,' the Doctor agreed. 'The Galactic Alliance is a neutral body, bit like the United Nations,' he went on quietly to Martha. 'They have control of the castle now.'

'Why?' she whispered back.

'Because whoever controls Castle Extremis controls the whole region. It's right slap-bang in the middle of the only safe route through this area. So give it to a neutral power and occupy it with a peacekeeping force and – fingers crossed...'

'Peace treaty?'

He nodded. 'The castle is at the head of the Sarandon Passage. Anthium one side of the divide, Zerugma the other. If either side wants to rule over its neighbour, it has to control Castle Extremis. The treaty is to formalise the peace, and officially hand over Extremis to the GA.'

'So they can make it into a theme park?'

'That's right. What a plan, eh? Just think of what could have happened if North and South Korea had decided to ditch their weapons programmes and buy Alton Towers instead. The soldiers of the Ninth Legion could have slept safely on their bunks if only Hadrian had opened his wall to tourists and charged a modest fee to walk along it and sketch pictures.'

'You reckon?'

The Doctor sucked air through his teeth and considered. 'Well, maybe. History is all about maybes.'

There were sentries outside the double doors at the end of the passage. Their armour looked more streamlined and modern than the costume – or the real thing – that Martha had seen. It was like a cross between modern combat gear and the sort of padding worn for American Football. The two men snapped to attention as Defron approached. He ignored them and strode into the room.

'I am pleased to announce that the GA Observation Team has arrived,' he said, and gestured for the Doctor and Martha to enter.

'Hi,' the Doctor said amiably.

Martha raised a hand in greeting. She didn't say anything, because she was too busy looking at the people sitting round the horseshoe-shaped conference table that dominated the room.

Defron made his way to a seat at the midpoint of the crescent. There were two spare seats at one end, and Martha followed the Doctor as he headed for one of them.

'So,' the Doctor said. 'I'm the Doctor and this is Martha. Why don't you take a quick moment to introduce yourselves, and then you can just carry on as if we're not here. How's that sound?'

Apart from Defron, there were four other people sitting at the table. An elderly lady with snow-white hair, a middle-aged man with broad shoulders and flint-hard eyes, and two crocodiles. A crocodile turned to look at Martha. One reptilian eye glittered, while the other was covered by a black patch. The ends of a livid white scar emerged from above and below the eyepatch. The creature's scales glistened as it turned, catching the light, and a string of pale saliva dripped from its jaws as sharp white teeth snapped together.

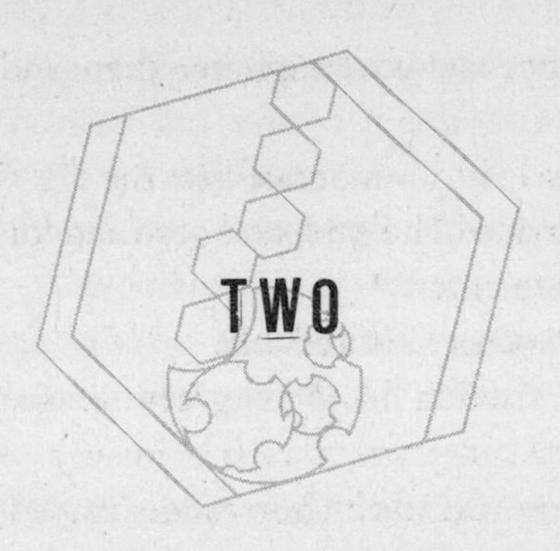

TWO

The old lady spoke first. Her voice was quiet and kindly as she looked at the Doctor and Martha across the curved table.

'I am Lady Casaubon, acting as personal representative of the President of Anthium. I am authorised to make any decision I deem necessary on his behalf.' She had the quiet confidence of a woman who was secure in her authority. She nodded to one of the crocodiles sitting opposite her across the horseshoe of the table.

It was not the one with the eyepatch. This crocodile-man looked older. His eyes were cloudy and some of his scales were broken and ragged. His teeth and the claws at the end of his green fingers were yellowed. His voice started as a low rasp somewhere right at the back of his throat. When he finally spoke, his voice was low and guttural, but surprisingly cultured.

'First Secretary Chekz of the Zerugian delegation. Like Lady Casaubon, I have full authority in these discussions. Like Lady Casaubon, I trust that we shall come to a sensible agreement and establish a lasting peace between our two great provinces.'

Lady Casaubon smiled and nodded appreciatively, and Chekz turned his jutting face towards the other Zerugian.

'I am General Orlo.' There was a brutal edge to the Zerugian's voice. The scales round his eyepatch twitched as he spoke, his voice deeper and more abrupt than the First Secretary's. 'I am here to assist Secretary Chekz and to advise in particular on military and strategic matters. That is all.' He leaned back in his chair and turned away, as if the matter was completely closed.

Defron cleared his throat politely. 'I think the General is doing himself a disservice,' he said. There was a low grunt from the General as Defron went on: 'General Orlo, as well as being Supreme Commander of the Zerugian Forces and a veteran of the unfortunate Tenth Conflict, is also a noted historian. He brings welcome context to these negotiations.'

'Good for you,' the Doctor declared, and clapped his hands several times. When no one else joined in, he shrugged and tipped back on his chair. 'Ignore me. That's fine.'

Lady Casaubon cleared her throat. 'General Orlo has also been good enough to furnish these discussions – quite literally to furnish Castle Extremis – with a quite splendid gift.' She turned towards Orlo, who was inspecting the ends of his claws as if the discussions were about someone else, someone he didn't really like.

'What gift is that?' Martha found herself asking. The General didn't look like the sort who'd turn up to the party with lavish presents wrapped in pink ribbon.

'As you know, we are restoring Castle Extremis to its former glory,' Defron said. 'One of the great treasures of the castle was the legendary Mortal Mirror. General Orlo has donated the most exquisite copy, which you probably saw in the Great Hall.'

Martha did remember the mirror. 'Yeah. Good stuff. Impressive.'

The Doctor sniffed. 'What happened to the original?'

The man beside Lady Casaubon answered. His lip curled slightly and his voice was heavy with sarcasm. 'It was lost, apparently destroyed, in the third Zerugian occupation. So I suppose it's only fair they provide a replacement.'

Orlo glared at the man, nostrils widening as a hint of steam emerged from them. 'There are other legends, other stories. Some say that after the Imprisonment, Governor Pennard had the mirror smashed to pieces.'

'And in so doing brought bad luck on Anthium and precipitated the Third Occupation,' the man said. 'I'm sure you're right. It all sounds very plausible to me.' He smiled suddenly, though his eyes remained hard and cold. 'Perhaps we should get Professor Thorodin back in to give us his opinion. Or perhaps not,' he added, feigning a yawn. 'We'd be here all night.'

'Professor *Millan* Thorodin?' the Doctor said.

Defron nodded. 'Noted expert on the Conflicts, and of course the legends of the Mortal Mirror. You know him?'

The Doctor shook his head. 'Never heard of him. Lucky guess.'

The man with the flint-hard eyes laughed.

'And I didn't catch your name?' the Doctor said to him.

'Stellman.'

'Just Stellman?' Martha asked.

The man shrugged his broad shoulders. 'I am not an aristocrat. Merely a humble citizen. So yes, just Stellman.'

'Stellman is my aide and adviser,' Lady Casaubon said. She sounded slightly apologetic. 'Though it seems that once again *I* must advise *him* – to keep his sarcasm and what passes for humour in check and show due respect.'

Stellman bowed his head. 'I consider myself so advised, My Lady,' he said contritely. 'Apologies, General. No offence.'

General Orlo did not reply.

'We-ell,' the Doctor said eventually in the silence that followed. 'I can see you all have lots to talk about and we don't want to slow you down. So if it's no problem we'll leave you to it for the moment and have a mooch round.'

Defron frowned. 'Mooch round?'

'Explore,' the Doctor explained, leaping to his feet. 'Go for a look-see, have a wander, take a gander. You know. We'll pop back and see how you're doing later.'

'Gonfer is preparing accommodation for you,' Defron said. 'I'll signal him to show you round.'

'Is he the silent monk?' Martha wondered.

'When he isn't a rather unconvincing Zerugian or a palace guard,' Stellman said.

'And he's not allowed to talk?' the Doctor asked.

'Correct,' Defron confirmed.

'Going to be some tour,' Martha said.

The monk met them in the corridor.

'Gonfer?' the Doctor asked.

The monk nodded, hood bowing forwards. Even when he straightened up again his face was hidden in shadow.

'That's good,' the Doctor went on. 'Thought I'd better check. After all, you've been Gonfer a while.' He sighed as he caught Martha's expression. 'Well, maybe not.'

Gonfer showed the Doctor and Martha to their rooms. It was hard to tell if he was surprised that they just glanced inside and had no luggage to leave.

'Nice,' the Doctor said, from the doorway of his room. 'Very nice. Now, what about that tour Defron promised us?'

It was a rather strange tour, their guide not saying a word and responding to their questions with just a nod or shake of the head. Or rather, of the hood as Martha couldn't see his face at all. For the most part it was like wandering round a well-preserved but rather boring castle anywhere in Britain, Martha thought.

Until they went outside.

'Oh my...' Martha's voice faded as she gazed up at the sky. 'I didn't – you never said... I mean...' She turned to the Doctor. 'We're in space.'

'Well, yes. I told you – guarding the Sarandon Passage.'

'Those of us who didn't take Galactic Geography and didn't realise this is all some sort of special space-stone and not whatever they usually build castles out of might have thought that was just like a valley or a mountain pass or something.'

'Might they?' The Doctor considered this. 'Might they really?'

'Yes. Really.'

'It's not.'

'I can see that now, thanks. I just – well, some sort of warning that we're floating through space might have helped.'

'Not floating,' the Doctor told her. 'Not really. Well, not as such. And it's built of stone because it used to be a monastery,' he added. As if that made more sense.

But Martha wasn't really listening. She was staring out across the courtyard. Above the battlements of the castle, a red and orange nebula spun slowly and majestically. Stars burned and asteroids hung impossibly close.

'Force field?' she said quietly. 'Keeping the air in?'

'Semi-permeable bubble,' the Doctor said. 'It keeps the atmosphere in, and only lets ships enter if they're going at less than three micro-spegs. Anything faster – like a missile, say – and: Bang!' he mimed an explosion by clapping and separating his hands. He made the noises too.

'So we're not going to suffocate or spin off into space then?'

'Doubt it.'

Martha smiled. 'Just checking.'

'Getting out is a bit easier – you can go faster and just stretch the bubble till you burst out. Concave rather than convex, you see.' He curled his hand to show her. 'Or is it the other way round? Never can remember. Still, doesn't matter.' The Doctor put his arm round Martha's shoulder and pointed at a glowing blue star that looked close enough to reach out and touch. 'That's Plastiocron. Beyond it – that pale shimmer you can just see – is the Colondian Rift.'

The monk – Gonfer was nodding and pointing too.

'The Aranning Nebula,' the Doctor agreed. 'Beautiful, isn't it?'

It was a shame to go back indoors, but eventually Gonfer led the Doctor and Martha across the courtyard and back into the castle through another door. Above them, on the battlements, Martha could see men in the same armour as those outside the conference room. Looking out into space, keeping watch.

She glanced back the way they had come, treating herself to one last look at the incredible view. A shadow moved, right in the middle of the courtyard. It darted suddenly to a darker patch where the starlight was shadowed by one of the huge towers rising up above them. Martha watched for a few moments, but saw nothing more. Just a shadow. A trick of the light. Nothing.

But – just for a moment – Martha had been sure it was a little girl.

The place was a mess. It looked like it was still being built, Martha thought. There were piles of stone stacked up by the walls of the wide corridor. Tiles were missing from the floor. An arched doorway was only half built – the stonework crude and unfinished.

Gonfer was holding his hands out. He bunched them into fists and mimed hammering one on top of the other.

'How many syllables?' the Doctor asked. 'Nah, only joking,' he went on quickly. 'Still building this bit?'

The monk's hood shook slightly.

'No – restoring it then?'

Gonfer nodded.

'What's with the monk-y business anyway?' Martha wanted to know.

'Castle Extremis was originally built as a monastery by the Mystic Mortal Monks of Moradinard,' the Doctor said, like everyone knew that. 'Before either Anthium or Zerugma realised the other was there and started fighting over the place.'

By the time he finished speaking, the Doctor was having to shout to be heard over the sound of a drill coming from the other side of the unfinished archway. He led the way through, Martha close behind. She was vaguely aware of a thudding sound behind her. Probably the monk, Gonfer, had tripped on the uneven floor. She didn't embarrass him by turning to watch.

Also, she was distracted by what she saw in the room. It was stripped back to the bare stone – much of it crumbling away. One wall had been refaced with new, smooth stone. Another was half complete. Two workmen were just finishing cutting along the edges of an old piece of stone and were lifting it away ready to replace it.

Two robot workmen. They were both vaguely humanoid, but neither would ever be mistaken for a man. One was tall and thin, with ball and socket joints oozing oil. It had metal prongs for hands that were easing under the stone like a fork-lift. The other robot was shorter and broad. It looked like it had been bolted together out of plates of rusty metal. Its hands were armoured gloves as it took the lump of stone from its fellow and swivelled at the waist to set it down on a pile of old, discarded rubble.

'So I said to him,' the tall thin robot was saying in a high-pitched nasal voice, 'I said – do you expect us to work for nothing? Give us credit.' Reedy laughter echoed off the bare stone walls. 'Give us *credit*.'

'Very good. Yes,' the shorter robot rumbled. 'Nice one, Bill.'

'Thank you, Bott. And though I say so myself, you're right.'

They paused as they saw the Doctor and Martha watching them.

'We're doing it, all right,' the tall thin robot – Bill – said quickly.

'We're doing it now. Straight away,' Bott agreed. 'Just as soon as—'

'Doing what?' the Doctor asked.

'That… thing. What you wanted doing,' Bill said. 'Everyone's full of orders and loads more seem to get downloaded from the GA all the time. Report on this, give us status on that. You know.'

'Oh, right. That,' the Doctor said. 'That *thing*. Good, that's good. Isn't that good, Martha?'

'It's great,' she agreed. 'Only we didn't want anything doing, thanks.'

There was silence. Bill looked at Bott and Bott looked at Bill. Then they both turned and looked at the Doctor and Martha.

'That's a first,' Bott said. 'Someone who doesn't want anything doing.'

'Unique,' Bill agreed. 'Usually it's mend this or polish that.'

'Stick this behind there. Take down that picture. Put up this mirror.'

'Mirror?' the Doctor asked.

'Might be a mirror,' Bott said. 'Or anything really. I was being hypothetical.'

'Did you put up the Mortal Mirror?' Martha asked.

Bill laughed his thin reedy laugh. 'How long do you think we've been here?'

'For ever,' Bott muttered. 'As you well know.'

Bill's laughter died. 'Yes, well, actually we did put it up. That was only a hundred years ago. We've been maintenance and renovation since before the monks left.'

'And it was their mirror, after all,' Bill went on. 'At least, it wasn't because it was after their time. But it was named after them. Mortal Monks – Mortal Mirror. There's a sort of reflection there. Get it? Reflection?!'

The two of them shook with electronic laughter.

'I think Martha meant the replica mirror, actually,' the Doctor said. 'That just arrived. With General Orlo.'

'Oh that, yeah,' Bott said. 'Don't know about *replica* though.'

'Looks just like the real one,' Bill agreed.

The Doctor nodded. 'That is sort of the point of a replica.' He walked over to where they were working and inspected the new stonework. 'This is very good – excellent workmanship. Or work-robot-ship I suppose, strictly speaking.'

'Only the very best,' Bott said proudly.

'Quality takes time though,' Bill said. 'Not a lot of people appreciate that.'

'Oh I do,' the Doctor told them. 'So does Martha. And Gonfer there too.'

Martha turned and saw that the monk was standing close behind her. She smiled at the dark space under the hood, and thought she saw a gleam of reflected light inside.

'Must be interesting,' the Doctor was saying. 'You do all the work – everything?'

'Course we do. We're programmed in masonry, stonemasonry, metalwork, carpentry,' Bill said proudly.

'Glazing, gardening, fixing, smithing and French polishing,' Bott went on. 'Though I'm expecting an upgrade patch for that any day now.'

'Not before time,' Bill muttered.

'Isn't it a bit boring?' Martha wondered. 'I mean, if you just keep repairing the same things and replacing them over and over again down the years?'

'Might be if we'd built the place,' Bill conceded. 'But we weren't here then. So there's some bits that keep needing doing.'

'Vacuuming,' Bott said.

'Cleaning the silver,' Bill said. 'But a lot of it we are getting to for the first time. First major renovation the place has ever had.'

'And well overdue at that,' Bott said.

'I guess there are some surprises then,' the Doctor said. 'I know in a lot of these old places the original builders and stonemasons left their own personal mark.'

'Like, carved their initials?' Martha said.

The Doctor nodded. 'Or even left things behind. You find it in cathedrals and churches, holy places mainly. You remove a panel, or lift out a stone...' He ran his hands over the old stone next to the gap where the robots had just been working. 'This one's loose, you see.'

The Doctor gripped the stone, easing his fingers into the gap behind and rocking it forwards until he could lift it out. 'And then, suddenly, when you're least expecting it, you find...'

He pulled the stone away. 'Well, in this case you don't find anything of course,' he said. 'Just hypothetical, like you said.' He dropped the heavy stone on the pile of rubble and dusted his hands together. 'But, you know, sometimes...' The Doctor frowned and peered into the hole where the stone had been.

Martha ran to look. 'What is it? Or are you mucking about?'

The Doctor reached into the hole and took something out. It was old and dusty – a package about the size of a sandwich, wrapped in old cloth. Martha sincerely hoped it wasn't a sandwich. Especially as the Doctor was now unwrapping it.

'That was lucky,' the Doctor said. 'I mean, what are the chances of just taking out a stone at random like that and finding...' He dropped the cloth to the floor. 'This.'

It was rectangular, smooth and dark like translucent, coloured plastic.

'Chances are pretty high if you put it there in the first place,' Bott said.

'Did you?' Martha asked.

'Not me,' Bott said.

'Nor me,' Bill added. 'Impressed the lady, though.'

'It's been there a long time,' the Doctor said. The top lifted, hinged along one side. Maybe it was a box. 'Is it plastic? How long ago was that stone put there, would you say?'

'I'd say 100 years, 3 months and 6 days,' Bill told them. 'Give or take an hour or so.'

'It's not plastic,' the Doctor said. 'Too brittle, too delicate, too cold.' He lifted it up and tentatively touched it with the tip of his tongue. 'Glass. Very old, tinted glass.'

At first Martha thought there was another glass lid under the first as the Doctor lifted that too. Then she realised: 'It's a book.'

'A book with glass pages.' The Doctor held it up to the light. 'Something there, written on it. Not a language I know or understand.'

'Or the TARDIS? Shouldn't it translate the text for us?'

'Doesn't seem to have done.' The Doctor closed the book and held it out to the monk, standing close by them now. 'Any ideas, Gonfer?'

The monk's hand glinted strangely as it whipped out to grab the book.

The Doctor pulled it away. 'Careful. It's old, brittle. Fragile.'

The monk lashed out again.

Again the Doctor kept the book out of reach. 'What's the matter with you?'

'Gonfer?' Martha reached for the hood of his cloak.

The monk turned quickly, and pushed her away. Then ran from the room.

The Doctor ran after him, Martha close behind. She reached the arched doorway in time to see the monk disappearing into the castle courtyard. But the Doctor wasn't following. He was helping a young man with brown hair and freckles to his feet.

The young man looked confused and embarrassed. He was rubbing the back of his head, and he appeared to be dressed only in long underwear.

'What happened?' the man said. 'Doctor?'

The Doctor looked at Martha.

'You know who he is?' Martha said to the man.

'Course I do, Martha.'

'And you are?' the Doctor prompted.

'Gonfer. I'm your guide – remember? Look, sorry, but who hit me? And why did they take my costume?'

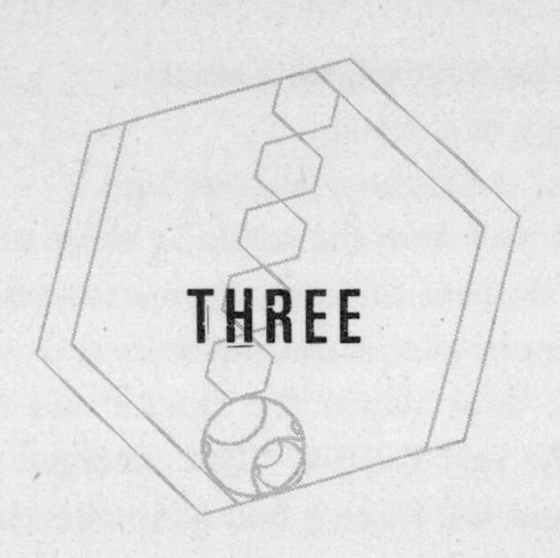

THREE

The Doctor left Martha to check the young man was all right, and ran back out into the courtyard. The light from the nebula and the stars cast long, spiky shadows across the ground and up the walls. The four towers at the corners of the castle were stark silhouettes against the almost-black sky.

There was more light coming from outside the castle – through the main arched gateway. Artificial sunlight, by the look of it. He ran towards the gatehouse, since it was as good a direction as any. There was no sign of the pretend monk. Or rather, he thought as he ran, the fake pretend monk.

He could see before he reached the gatehouse that a paved pathway led out of the castle and down into ornate gardens – gravel paths criss-crossing between rolling lawns, a formal rose garden, lakes and trees and what might even have been a maze.

But no sign of a monk.

'Lost him,' the Doctor said out loud.

'He went back into the castle,' a voice said from the shadows at the base of the gatehouse towers. 'That way.' The girl stepped out of the shadows and pointed back towards the door where the Doctor and Martha and Gonfer – the real Gonfer – had emerged earlier. The same little girl the Doctor had seen when he came out of the TARDIS.

'Do you know who he was?'

'Mortal Monk.'

'Not a real monk, not even a pretend real monk,' the Doctor told her. 'But to reuse a well-worn old joke, he was certainly up to monk-y business.'

The girl laughed. She looked about twelve years old, with straggly blonde hair and a face smudged with dirt. Her clothes were little better than rags, but she looked well enough fed.

'I'm the Doctor,' the Doctor said. 'You saw me earlier. You've been following us, haven't you – me and my friend Martha. Why's that?'

The girl shrugged. 'You're new. You're funny.'

The Doctor grinned. 'Yeah. Both those things. So, what's your name?'

'Today I'm called Janna.'

'That's a good name. Don't think I've met a Janna before. Do you have another name on other days?'

The girl looked away. When she looked back, her

smile had gone and she looked suddenly even younger, more vulnerable. 'Bye,' she said before the Doctor could speak. Then she ran through the gateway and down into the garden, skipping along one of the paths.

'Bye, Janna,' the Doctor called after her.

The girl turned and waved, before running on into the distance.

It seemed that Gonfer was allowed to talk if he wasn't actually wearing his monk's costume. Now, somewhat embarrassed, he was leading the Doctor and Martha through the castle to the servants' quarters. He had been rather wary of Martha checking his head to make sure he wasn't too badly hurt, and waving her fingers in front of him while she checked he wasn't concussed. So she could imagine he didn't feel entirely at ease walking through the castle dressed only in his undies.

'It gets so hot in that cowl,' he'd tried to explain.

'That's all right,' the Doctor said easily. 'Don't mind us. Well, don't mind me. You might want to mind Martha. Up to you, really.'

'I promise not to stare,' Martha said solemnly.

'And this would be the most deserted route to the servants' quarters, would it?' the Doctor enquired innocently.

'Stop teasing him,' Martha whispered.

'I was just saying.'

'Well, don't. Can't you see how embarrassed he is about all this?'

The Doctor grinned and raised his eyebrows. 'Oh yes.' Then suddenly he was serious again. 'You didn't see who clonked you on the bonce then?'

Gonfer shook his head, then looked like he wished he hadn't.

'It's all right, you can talk when you're not wearing your habit,' Martha said.

'So,' the Doctor said, 'why do you suppose someone would want to nick your costume?'

'Disguise?' Martha suggested. 'You can't see who's inside those things.'

'Good thought, good thought. But why do they need a disguise?' The Doctor weighed the glass book in his hands as they walked on. 'He was interested in this, wasn't he? But he couldn't have known we were about to find it any more than we did.'

'He or she,' Martha pointed out.

'Or *it*,' the Doctor added encouragingly. 'Not a Zerugian, their teeth stick out. And their noses, snouts – whatever.'

'Robot, like Bill and Bott?' Martha suggested.

'There aren't any other robots,' Gonfer said.

They arrived at Gonfer's room, and he left them on the landing outside while he went in to find some clothes.

'Someone watching us, you think?' Martha asked while they were alone. 'You saw a little girl when we arrived. I saw her too, in the courtyard.'

The Doctor nodded. 'Too small to inhabit the habit. She was still in the courtyard. Her name's Janna.'

Gonfer came out of his room in time to hear this. Martha was relieved to see he'd put on loose trousers and collarless shirt and not another silent-monk outfit.

'You met Janna?' Gonfer asked

'Best mates, me and Janna,' the Doctor told him. 'Who is she, by the way?'

But Gonfer didn't seem to hear. He was too busy rubbing his head again and groaning. 'I could do with a lie down,' he said after a moment. 'I'll take you back to the negotiating chamber, if that's all right. They'll be breaking for lunch soon.'

'Good, I'm starving,' Martha said. She hadn't realised it till a few minutes ago, but she couldn't remember when she'd last eaten anything.

'Ah, I was hoping for a tour of the gardens,' the Doctor said with exaggerated disappointment.

Gonfer shook his head. 'Best ask someone else.'

'Not your specialist subject?'

'It's a minefield out there.'

The Doctor nodded sympathetically. 'All those different types of plant to remember, finding your way through the maze, not losing anyone in the duck pond. Yes I can see that.'

'No, really,' Gonfer said. 'It's a minefield. With anti-personnel mines, and mantraps and everything. Defences left over from the war, in case of incursion. That's how Janna's sister...' He broke off. 'We can cut through the Long Gallery, there are some interesting paintings there.'

The Doctor and Martha looked at each other.

'Tell us about Janna,' the Doctor said quietly. 'And tell us what happened to her sister.'

They stood on the battlements, overlooking the formal gardens laid out below. Tall lighting rigs blazed artificial sunlight across the lawn making it look like a football ground. Martha and the Doctor leaned out to see better.

Martha found it hard to believe that the beauty and elegance she was looking at was tainted by hidden death traps. Beyond the lawn she could see a lake, and there were formal gardens too, with flowerbeds and low hedges. To the side of the gatehouse she could see the higher hedges of a maze and just make out some of the paths inside.

In the distance, beyond the lake and the lawns, the world just stopped. The lights reached to the broken edge of the grounds, and beyond it the night sky was full of stars. It was as if some cosmic giant had bitten the end off the world, leaving just a ragged edge hanging impossibly in space...

'They were born here,' Gonfer said. 'Janna, and her sister – her twin sister.'

'What was her sister's name?' Martha had gathered that the sister was no longer around.

'Tylda. Janna and Tylda. No one could tell them apart, at least, not by looking at them.'

'By temperament?' the Doctor wondered.

'Oh yes. Though even so it was difficult to tell for sure

which was which. One of them – Janna – was happy and bright and clever and helpful. She'd work in the kitchens or with Bill and Bott. Nothing was too much trouble.'

'Tylda was different?'

'They were opposites. Her sister was surly and stubborn. She'd do nothing to help – just run off. One was polite and sympathetic. The other, well, she teased and insulted and bullied...' Gonfer turned away, his eyes moist.

'Did she insult you?' Martha asked quietly.

Gonfer nodded. He wiped his eyes. 'I hated her. *Really* hated her. She was only, what – about ten or eleven? But she could be so nasty. Evil. No,' he said at once, correcting himself. 'Not evil, that's too harsh. But she was unpleasant and she enjoyed upsetting people.'

'Where did they come from, these girls?'

'Oh, now that's a good question,' the Doctor said. 'Excellent question, that. Wish I'd thought of it. Actually, I did,' he remembered.

'They were always here,' said Gonfer. 'Born here. Their mother worked in the castle. Not sure exactly what she did. It was well before I arrived.'

'And their father?' the Doctor asked.

'Mother died soon after the twins were born. Father was a guard with the Anthium Heavy Infantry, I think. Well, twelve years ago – you can guess.'

'But the war was over by then, wasn't it? Or at least, they'd stopped fighting over this place.'

The Doctor glanced at Martha. 'Tell us anyway.'

'He was posted to the Ursuline Fringes. Killed at Modolfin in the reactor accident, like all the others.'

'And the girls stayed here, Janna and Tylda?' Martha said. 'They just got left behind?'

'I think officially they were left in the care of the Adjutant of Extremis. But he couldn't care less about them. Or anything else, come to that.'

'What happened to him?' Martha asked.

Gonfer shook his head. 'He's still here. Well, he isn't because he went off in a huff when Defron set up the treaty negotiations and didn't involve him, thank goodness. Said he'd got six months leave owing and he was taking it. Probably cruising round Hamthis drunk out of his mind on booster tabs.'

'And what,' the Doctor asked quietly, 'happened to Tylda?'

Gonfer leaned back against the wall, staring past the Doctor and Martha. 'She'd annoy the guards, the kitchen staff, anyone. They got so riled they'd chase her off, and she'd run away laughing. Into the garden. She knew no one would dare to follow her there.'

Martha felt suddenly cold. 'You said the garden was a minefield.'

'Not all of it.' Gonfer pointed to the long swathes of beautifully cut grass. 'The lawns are cut with mecho-mowers which won't trigger the mines because they aren't organic. They've been adapted to prune the hedges and other stuff. But the girls, they knew the safe ways through the garden.'

'Still do,' the Doctor said. 'Janna ran off into the garden after I spoke to her. Just along there.' He pointed. 'Good job I didn't follow.'

Gonfer nodded. 'Most of the mines have been cleared now, under the auspices of the GA. The paths are all clear now, or so they tell us. But I'm not convinced. When you've seen what those things can do… Anyway, they reckon a death trap wouldn't be too good for the tourists they hope will come.'

'Probably not,' the Doctor agreed.

'But it was very different a year ago' said Gonfer. 'I think the girls learned where was safe from the gardeners. They keep themselves to themselves, and they never go near the lawns. But some of the jobs need real people to do them still. Maybe they have maps of where the mines are or something, I don't know.' He paused, biting his lower lip before going on with his story. 'Tylda upset one of the kitchen boys. *Really* upset him. He was shouting and screaming at her. I'll never forget it. She ran away…'

'And of course she ran away into the garden,' the Doctor said.

Gonfer turned, unable to look down into the gardens as he spoke. 'She must have strayed from the safe path across the lawn. The explosion was heard right through the castle. It blew out the windows in the East Wing below us.'

'So Janna's on her own, poor thing,' the Doctor said quietly.

'Oh no,' Gonfer told him. 'She's changed. She doesn't help now. She hides in the shadows and creeps round the castle like she's a ghost. She steals food from the kitchens, though of course they don't mind. They feel sorry for her – like we all do.'

'Sounds like she's on her own to me,' Martha said.

'She still has Tylda with her,' Gonfer said. 'It's like they've fused together. If you talk to her, you never know which of the twins you're with. She might be quiet and polite and helpful. The next moment she's raging and angry and insulting. It's like her dead sister is somehow inside her body, with her.'

The Doctor tapped his fingers on the top of the wall. 'Result of the trauma. She's become a sort of introvert, who can't let go. Twins can be bound very tightly together.'

'One person, but two aspects?' Martha said.

'Sometimes angelic – like when she spoke to me. Sometimes mischievous.'

'Like when she tried to lead you into the minefield,' Martha said.

'I wouldn't say it's all safe,' Gonfer told them. 'But stick to the paths and they say you'll be OK. And Janna knows the safe routes better than anyone. She's mischievous not murderous. I think.'

'Well,' the Doctor said, 'that's comforting to know.'

Plates of cold meat and bowls of salad had been laid out on the main table in the Great Hall. But Professor

Thorodin ignored it. He was standing in front of the Mortal Mirror when Lady Casaubon arrived.

Hearing her footsteps on the stone floor, Thorodin turned and walked swiftly to collect a pile of books and papers he had left on a side table.

'You are alone, Professor?' Lady Casaubon asked in surprise.

'Evidently.'

'I thought I heard voices.'

'Just me,' the Professor confessed. 'I was making some notes. I read them aloud as I write sometimes. When I'm alone.'

'Forgive me for disturbing you,' Lady Casaubon said. 'The others will be here shortly if you wish to join us for lunch. Defron is clarifying a point of order with Chekz. I'm afraid it went over my head rather. But join us, please. You will be very welcome.'

Thorodin picked up his books and papers. 'Thank you, My Lady. I should put these away.'

'I hope the Doctor and Martha will join us too,' Lady Casaubon added as she walked up to gaze into the large mirror at the end of the room. 'It is so very fine,' she said quietly. 'And so unusually generous for General Orlo to make such a gift.'

'General Orlo is an unusual individual,' Thorodin said. 'Who are the Doctor and Martha?' he went on. 'I don't think I've had the pleasure.'

Lady Casaubon wrinkled her nose and raised her eyebrows, examining her reflection in the looking glass.

'GA observers. They seem harmless enough, if a little...' She shrugged, unsure what the word was. Thorodin was standing too far to the side of the room for her to see him in the mirror, so she turned. 'You will join us?'

'I'd be glad to.' Thorodin had his books and papers balanced on his right forearm, steadying them with his left hand. 'I'll see you soon.'

As he left, Lady Casaubon turned back to her reflection. So many lines and wrinkles, she thought. She didn't resent them – experience and wisdom came with a price. She could still see the young woman she had once been – the young woman she still felt she was, really – in her reflected image. But could anyone else? She smiled sadly, and her reflection smiled back at her.

Gonfer led the way down the steps from the battlements into the courtyard. They were steep and, despite the huge lights shining on the gardens outside the walls, they were soon in shadow. Martha carefully watched where she was putting her feet. She didn't fancy tumbling down the aged steps, knocking the Doctor and Gonfer flying.

'Why make such beautiful gardens a death trap?' she wondered aloud. It seemed such a shame that the gardens were there but couldn't be enjoyed.

'I think it's the other way round,' the Doctor called back over his shoulder. 'This was a fortress, remember. They mined the area outside the walls in case anything got through the force bubble thing.'

'Weaker at the edges,' Martha remembered.

'That's right. If you have to look out over a deadly minefield death trap area, well – no reason not to make it look pretty.'

'I suppose.' Martha wasn't convinced that made it any better.

'And it'd confuse the hell out of the enemy. They might even get lost in the maze.'

By the time Martha reached the bottom of the steps, the Doctor and Gonfer were already striding out across the courtyard, deep in conversation. Or, at least, deep in the Doctor monologuing and Gonfer looking confused.

Martha sighed and set off quickly after them. Then she stopped, and turned. She'd felt a prickling at the back of her neck like someone was watching her. Sure enough, there was a figure standing in the shadows beside the base of the steps. A girl.

'You Martha?' the girl asked.

'That's right,' Martha said.

'You don't want to listen to Gonfer,' the girl said. 'He's a peasant.'

'Really?'

The girl shrugged. 'I don't like him. He's stupid.'

Martha nodded. 'He was telling me about you and your sister,' she said.

The girl's eyes narrowed. 'What did he say? It's all lies.' Her face was blank, like a mask. Like she was suppressing all feeling and thought and emotion.

'Janna and Tylda,' Martha said, watching the girl's expression. It didn't change. 'Which one are you?'

On the other side of the courtyard the Doctor and Gonfer paused at the door and glanced back, looking to see where Martha had got to.

Neither of them noticed the cowled figure that stood nearby, watching them silently from the shadows.

In the reflection of the Great Hall, Lady Casaubon could see the food prepared for lunch. She turned, deciding which of the meats to start with. Diplomacy might be a dreadful bore, but at least one was well fed.

Behind her, Lady Casaubon's reflection had not turned. It watched the elderly woman surveying the food. Its expression had changed from a sad smile to a cruel sneer. It reached out a wrinkled hand, pushed it through the mirror. The glass rippled round the fingers, the wrist, the elbow as the reflection reached out of the looking glass. The clawed fingers slowly edged towards Lady Casaubon's shoulder.

The reflection stepped forward. A foot broke the surface of the mirror. A wrinkled face pushed through, as if surfacing through water. The hand descended towards the old woman's unsuspecting shoulder.

'Lady Casaubon?' The shout came from outside the Great Hall. 'My Lady – are you there?'

Lady Casaubon sighed and walked quickly towards the door. 'I'm here, Stellman,' she replied. 'I am more than ready for lunch.'

Stellman appeared in the doorway. 'I'm sorry, My Lady. I didn't see you leave.' The concern faded from his face. 'If I had, I would have left myself. Defron is such a pedant. And as for Orlo…'

They smiled at each other. A private moment of amusement and honesty in the midst of the tact and diplomacy.

And the old lady in the mirror cursed silently as she stepped away from the reflection and back into the shadows of the world behind the mirror.

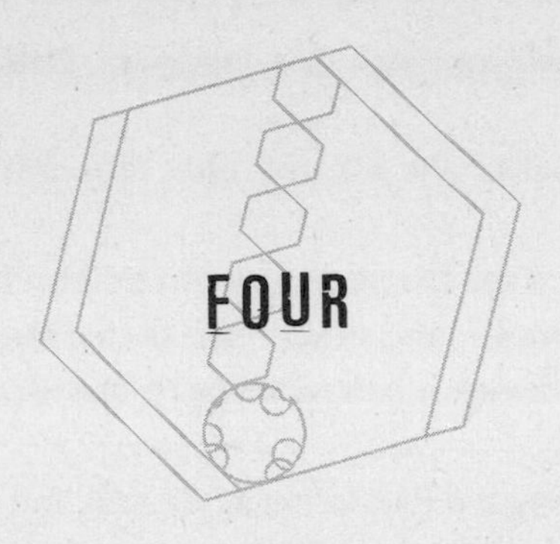

FOUR

Lunch was a surprisingly informal event. Gonfer led the Doctor and Martha back to the Great Hall.

'See you later,' Martha said.

The Doctor leaned close to Gonfer and whispered: 'And if it's just us, you can talk. Even in costume. We won't tell. Scout's honour.'

The slight figure of Defron hurried over to them and enthused about the food. 'Though I'd avoid the Zerugian water truffles,' he said in a low voice. 'They're only here because we know that General Orlo likes them.'

'Not good?' Martha said.

Defron shook his head. 'They're the things that look like fetid pond weed. Well, actually, from talking to the chef, I've discovered that they *are* fetid pond weed.'

'Definitely trying that,' the Doctor decided, grabbing a clean plate and napkin from the end of the table.

'Please tell me he's not serious,' Defron said to Martha.

'Not usually,' she assured him. 'But this time, who knows?'

She joined the Doctor in time to see him fishing what did indeed look – and smell – like fetid pond weed from a large bowl with a pair of tongs. It was straggly, green and mushy.

'I'm hoping it's like spinach,' he said, not seeming to realise that everyone else had stopped to watch him.

Lady Casaubon was shaking her head at Martha in an attempted warning. Martha shook her head back, meaning 'He won't be told.' Stellman watched with a resigned expression on his face. Defron had his hand over his mouth. Chekz and Orlo stood on the opposite side of the table watching with interest.

The Doctor lifted a long strand of gooey green weed with his fingers and dangled it high above his mouth. 'Well, here goes.' He hesitated. 'Although, now I come to think about it, I don't really like spinach.' He sighed. 'Oh well.' And dropped the green stuff into his mouth.

Almost at once he doubled up. 'Oh,' he managed to say through a mouthful of weed. 'Oh cripes. Crikey O'Reilly. Gordon Bennett. Uncle Tom Cobley and all.'

He straightened up and shook his head violently, coughing.

'Are you all right?' Martha wasn't sure if he was choking.

'Oh, but that is *good*,' the Doctor announced. 'Really

good. You should try it Martha. What's that sort of spicy aftertaste?'

'The seed pods emit a mild acid when crushed,' Orlo told him.

'That's brilliant. Really brings out the flavour, doesn't it?' He started to ladle more of the mushy green weed onto his plate. 'You could put this in sandwiches, make soup, have it with chips. Oh yes. Can I get you some, Martha?'

'I think I'll pass, thanks. There's cheese and stuff over there.'

'Your loss,' the Doctor said indistinctly through another mouthful.

Martha kept to food she recognised. She was helping herself to a very safe-looking bread roll when Stellman came up to her.

'So how are things at the GA?'

'Oh, you know,' Martha said. 'Same as ever.'

'That bad?' Stellman asked, apparently in all seriousness.

Martha smiled through a bite of roll, just in case he was joking. She wasn't sure she'd seen the man smile. Maybe his face didn't do that. 'How are the negotiations going?' she asked. Adding a quick 'Sorry' as breadcrumbs sprayed across Stellman's suit.

He brushed them off without comment. 'Same as ever,' he said. And this time Martha was sure she saw a slight twitch in one eye. Perhaps he was joking after all.

On the other side of the table, General Orlo had

engaged the Doctor in animated conversation. Martha wasn't sure what it was about, but from the few words she caught, it seemed likely it was a discussion about the merits of the pond weed truffle stuff. She was better off talking to Stellman, she decided.

'It's an acquired taste,' a voice said.

Martha turned to find that First Secretary Chekz had joined them. 'Don't think I'll be acquiring it,' she told him. 'Sorry.'

The huge creature towered over Martha, but somehow he managed not to seem intimidating. Not like Orlo. 'There really is no obligation,' he said kindly. 'I think your friend is being polite.'

'You can take diplomacy too far,' Stellman said.

Chekz's head bobbed up and down and he made a rhythmic growling sound that Martha took to be laughter. 'I myself have never much taken to water truffles,' he said. 'But like the Doctor, I have found myself in situations where one must pretend.' He turned to Stellman. 'As you say, diplomacy. Tell me, do you think Lady Casaubon would back down on item five if I were to back down on the restitution clause?'

'I think you might find her sympathetic to such a suggestion,' Stellman said. 'Provided you made it clear you were also willing to reconsider the question of the settlers on the Gammantrilon Plateau.'

Chekz nodded. 'That may be possible. Perhaps I will suggest it now. While my colleague the good General is distracted.'

'You don't think he'd go for it?' Martha asked, though she didn't know what they were talking about.

'General Orlo gives way on nothing,' Chekz said. 'He sees all compromise as surrender.'

'So why is he here?'

It was Stellman who answered. 'Perhaps he thinks it is better that both sides surrender than risk the other side winning.'

'Or perhaps,' Chekz said, 'he is old and tired. I know I am. Now, please excuse me.' He lumbered across to where Lady Casaubon was talking quietly to Defron. Despite being a huge upright crocodile creature, Martha thought, he did indeed look frail. She wondered how long the Zerugian life span was, and turned to ask Stellman.

But before their conversation could progress, another man came into the room. He was tall and thin, walking with a slight stoop. His hair was grey and thinning badly on the top. He walked carefully and slowly round the edge of the room, as if keen to keep well away from the food.

'Looks like he's tried the water truffles,' Martha said quietly to Stellman.

'Professor Thorodin always looks like that,' Stellman told her.

'The mirror man?'

'Oh he's an expert in all manner of antiquities. Or so he keeps telling us.' Stellman called across: 'Professor, come and meet Miss Mouse.'

'Martha,' she corrected him quickly. She held out her hand to the Professor, but the man ignored it.

'I can't stop,' Thorodin said in an agitated and impatient tone. 'I had some questions about the replica mirror for General Orlo but he seems...'

He broke off to glance at Orlo who was still talking with the Doctor. At that moment the two of them burst into laughter.

'Oh that's good,' the Doctor was saying loudly. 'Very good. You ever heard of a guy called Noel Coward? Very funny, Noel.'

'... busy,' Thorodin finished, as the General clapped a clawed reptilian hand on the Doctor's shoulder and led him away from the table.

'You think the peace process will work?' the Doctor asked. Now he'd broken the ice with the General, and munched his way through some of the most revoltingly disgusting vegetation he'd ever tasted, he reckoned he was entitled to cut to the nitty-gritty.

The General's jaw moved slowly back and forth as he considered. 'It is working so far, but the process is of necessity long and drawn out.'

'These things always take time. Time for memories to fade and wounds to heal. You've come a long way in twenty years.'

'Too far for any of us to back out gracefully,' Orlo agreed. 'But that just makes it all the more dangerous.'

'I can't see Lady Casaubon throwing in the towel and

calling for the troops,' the Doctor said. He gave the old lady a friendly wave across the room.

'Yet Anthium sees fit to send Stellman to make sure she does not concede too much.'

'And Zerugma sends you,' the Doctor pointed out. 'A soldier. A general, no less. Highly decorated, no doubt.'

'No doubt,' Orlo growled. 'Stellman and I are similar, I grant you that. We both know the value of strength and power. We both, perhaps, yearn for the days when things were easier – us and them. Them and us.'

'Easier, but not safer.'

'Peace is not a natural state of affairs,' Orlo said. 'There is nothing inherently safe about peace. Better, surely, to be at war and know your enemies, know where the threat is coming from. A truce, however uneasy, is sometimes better than a surrender.'

'You see this as a surrender?'

'Both sides must surrender something. That is what negotiation is about. That is why we are here.'

Yes,' the Doctor said, 'but isn't it just a teensy-weensy bit about trust and friendship and making the universe a better place to live in?'

Orlo chuckled, saliva dripping from his lower jaw. 'As I said, Doctor, that is why we are here. If I did not believe – seriously believe – that what I am doing here is right, is the best course for my people, then I should not have come.'

'*Your* people?' The Doctor raised an eyebrow.

'A turn of phrase.'

'If peace comes,' the Doctor told Orlo, '*when* peace comes, I imagine you will be surrendering a lot. Personally. For your people.'

Orlo's deep red eye regarded the Doctor closely for a moment. Then he turned and pointed down the length of the table towards the enormous mirror that dominated the far end of the room. 'I have already shown I am willing to make sacrifices. That mirror is a replica of the original Mortal Mirror that hung there.'

'And very impressive it is too.'

'My great grandfather led the raiding party that took Extremis and destroyed the original mirror. He burned the wooden frame, and cast the shattered pieces of glass into space so it could never be reassembled.'

'Yet someone built a replica.'

'His son – my grandfather. He had it made as a reminder, lest we ever forget that we must only ever destroy in order to create. Out of war must come something positive, or else the war is not worth the cost. Out of war must come power, territory, wealth…'

'Peace?' the Doctor suggested.

Orlo turned back to him, his great scaly head nodding slowly. 'So it would seem.' His eye blinked as he looked past the Doctor. 'I see that Professor Thorodin has deigned to grace us with his presence. Why are clever men so often dull, Doctor? Are you wise enough to tell me that?'

'Oh I doubt it,' the Doctor said, turning to look at the stooped man walking slowly towards the doorway. 'But

I'm clever enough to know one thing.'

'And what is that?'

'That I'm the exception that proves the rule. Here, hold this a minute, will you?' The Doctor thrust his empty plate at Orlo. As the General took it, the Doctor turned, jumped up on to the table, hopscotched between the plates and dishes, and jumped down the other side.

'Never dull, me,' he called back to Orlo, running to catch the Professor before he reached the door.

'Are you the entertainment?' Thorodin asked drily as the Doctor ran up to him.

'Frequently. Just wanted to say hello. Professor Thorodin, isn't it? I read your paper on the origins of ancient Anthium and the Wandering Scholars. Terrific stuff. Just terrific. Mind you, completely wrong about the part played by Cranthus. I mean – what were you thinking of? What was that all about, eh?'

Thorodin's expression did not change. 'Is there some point to this, Doctor?'

'Oh, you've heard of me too?'

'Very recently. Are you published?'

'Published, translated, out of print – you name it. And talking of books, I wanted to ask you about this.'

The Doctor reached into his jacket pocket and took out the glass book he had found behind the stone. He leafed carefully through the brittle pages, showing it to Thorodin.

'Where did you get that?' the Professor asked, his voice barely more than a whisper.

'Found it. Behind a stone. Here in the castle. Interesting isn't it? I was wondering if you could tell me anything about it?'

'What makes you think I'd know anything?'

'Oh, because you're clever. And an expert on the history of Castle Extremis.'

Thorodin glared at the Doctor, then lifted the book carefully from him. He examined it closed, peering at the symbols on the pages. 'There is a system to this. It *is* writing. But not a language I know.'

'Code of some sort?'

'Possibly.'

'I can usually do codes. Quite good at them. But this...' The Doctor took the book back and ran his finger along a line of the enigmatic text. 'Something unworldly about it. Something "other". Something from outside time and space. Must be.'

'What makes you say that?' Thorodin asked slowly.

'Oh, nothing really. Just rambling. Ignore me.' The Doctor grinned. 'Well, thanks for your valuable time. Don't let me keep you.'

'You won't,' Thorodin assured him. 'But if you find out more...'

'Yes?'

'I would be interested.'

The Doctor walked slowly round the long table and back to Orlo.

'You were right,' he said. 'Not convinced about the clever. But he's certainly dull. Dull as ditchwater. Talking of which, is there any more of that truffle stuff left, or did we finish it all?'

First Secretary Chekz was about to leave the Zerugians' quarters when he heard a knock at the door. He put the papers he needed for the next session down on a table and opened the door. He was surprised to see the man standing outside.

'And how can I help *you*?' Chekz asked.

'I was looking for General Orlo,' the man said. 'I wanted a quick word. There are... developments.'

'What sort of developments? The General has already gone to the negotiating chamber. I should be leaving too.'

'Can I talk to you?'

'Anything you can tell Orlo, you can tell me.'

'Then – you know? You know of the General's plan?'

'Plan?' The scales round Chekz's eyes wrinkled.

'The mirror. The plan. There is a problem. It doesn't work as he thinks it does. I know – I am proof. Everything is so fragile. If he goes ahead, he has to...' The man hesitated, seeing Chekz's worried expression. 'You don't know at all, do you?'

'No,' Chekz agreed. 'But I think you had better tell me. Tell me everything.'

'I can't.' He turned to go.

Chekz caught the man's shoulder and pulled him back into the room. 'Tell me,' he insisted. 'I know the General's ambition, his feelings about these talks. And

I know that peace is the only hope we have – Zerugians and Anthiums.'

The man pulled himself free. 'Get off me. I'll talk only to Orlo, you old fool. You have no idea who I am, what you are doing. You don't recognise me at all. And you really think peace – *surrender* – is the answer?'

'Yes, I do,' Chekz said quietly. 'What do you mean, I don't recognise you?'

'My name is Sastrak,' the man said.

Chekz gasped and stepped back, his claws scraping on the stone floor. 'That can't be. How?'

'Orlo was right not to involve you. You are old and weak and *wrong*. There will be no peace.'

'Oh yes there will.' Chekz stepped forward again, reaching for the man. 'You will come with me, now. To the negotiations.' He grabbed the man's arm. 'We will ask Orlo to explain this plan in person.'

'Get off me!' the man insisted.

He wrenched his arm back, but Chekz held on. 'I said get off!' The man thrust the Zerugian away from him, but still Chekz held on. He dug his claws into the sleeve, but there was resistance. Strangely, the material did not yield.

Then they were falling as the man pushed again – hard. Chekz slipped backwards. The man's arm tore free of his grasp – and smashed into the side table, sending Chekz's papers flying.

Smashed.

The arm smashed.

Papers drifted down around the man as he raised his shattered arm in disbelief.

'What have you done?' he screamed. His hand lay splintered and broken on the floor close to where Chekz had fallen. The man's arm ended at the jagged wrist. The broken stump was sharp, with splinters and shards sticking out like thin bones.

Chekz stared at the hand lying on the floor. Stared at the broken wrist, the chipped fingers. The way it caught the light.

Then the man stabbed downwards with his broken arm. The sharp jagged end ripped through the First Secretary's tunic and into his cold flesh.

They heard the cry in the negotiating chamber. For a moment there was silence. No one moved.

Stellman and the Doctor recovered at the same instant, running for the door.

'Chekz,' Stellman said as they ran together. 'Along here.'

Martha caught up with them as they stood in the open doorway to the Zerugians' quarters.

'Job for you, Martha,' the Doctor said quietly.

She stepped past him, and knelt by the body. She reckoned a vet would be more use – she knew almost nothing about reptiles. But she had to do what she could. There was so much blood. Cold blood.

As she felt for the wound, tried to staunch the bleeding, Chekz gave a final gasp, and his head lolled to one side.

'Oh no,' Lady Casaubon said from the doorway. 'Is he...?'

'I'm sorry,' Martha said, her own voice as numb and flat and cold as she felt inside. 'We're too late.'

She lifted her hands away from the body and, as she did so, something caught the light, something sticking out of the wound. She pulled it out, grasping it with her handkerchief, careful not to cut herself on the sharp edges.

'What is that?' Defron asked as Martha held it up.

'It's glass,' the Doctor said.

Martha nodded. 'But why stab him with glass?'

'Stab him?' Defron's voice rose in pitch. 'At *my* conference? It must have been an accident. Some sort of grotesque, crazy accident.'

'I doubt it,' the Doctor said, crouching down beside Martha to examine the long, sharp sliver of glass.

'But why – how can you know it was deliberate?' Defron asked.

'The weapon detectors,' Stellman said quietly, 'do not scan for glass.'

No one said anything. They were all staring down at the body, at the blood, at the shard of broken glass. And they were all listening to the sound of rapid footsteps – the sound of a child, running quickly away from the room...

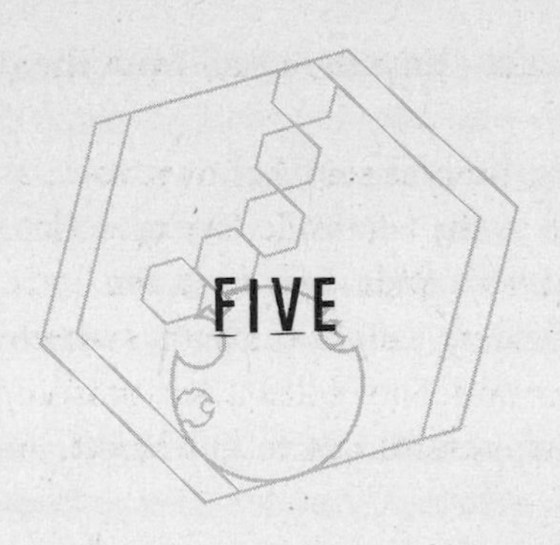

FIVE

'Keep an eye on things,' the Doctor whispered to Martha.

'Where are you going?'

'Cherchez la femme!' he announced, straightening up and running from the room.

'Well, really!' Defron complained as the Doctor nudged him aside. He seemed more put out at getting an elbow in the ribs than he did at Chekz getting stabbed in his.

'Should we get Hombard?' Stellman suggested. He was leaning against the wall, one hand in his jacket pocket.

'Is he a medic?' Martha asked. 'A doctor?'

'He's a chef,' Lady Casaubon said.

'But he's done the first-aid training,' Defron added quickly. 'The Health and Safety people insisted.'

Martha stared at them.

'I think we're a bit late for first aid, don't you?' she said. 'Look at him – he's dead. And I don't think there's much doubt about the cause of death.'

'There is every doubt,' General Orlo announced, pushing past the others into the room.

Martha held up the glass. '*This* was the cause of death. All right?'

'*That* is what killed him. It was the *means* not the cause,' Orlo growled. 'And we need to know the cause. Was he killed to sabotage our negotiations, or perhaps to help them? Or in a personal feud or – as Defron rather improbably suggested – in an accident? Was it suicide or murder?'

'Yeah, all right, I get the message,' Martha said. 'Look, we can't just leave him here.'

'Indeed we can't,' Orlo said. 'I will need to work here – if I am to prepare the Zerugian response to this outrage.' He turned slowly to glare at Lady Casaubon.

'You surely cannot believe—' Defron started.

But Orlo cut him off. 'I believe nothing. I deal only in facts. And the facts are plain. First Secretary Chekz refused to give way on certain key issues. Lady Casaubon was frustrated.'

Martha rolled her eyes. 'She's an old lady. I really don't see her taking on a seven-foot tall crocodile in single combat. Do you?'

'I don't think General Orlo meant Lady Casaubon,' Stellman said calmly. 'I think he believes – or perhaps merely suspects – that I killed Chekz.'

'And why would you do that?'

'Because Chekz was Zerugian and I am an Anthium. Because it might force a compromise in our current stalemate. Because I am the only one here strong enough...' Stellman shrugged. 'And because, by trade, I am an assassin.'

The sound of footsteps echoed back down the corridor. The Doctor was running to keep up. It was difficult to tell if he was gaining on the girl or not. But she couldn't be far ahead of him.

Which made it all the more surprising when he rounded a corner and saw that there was no sign of her in the long corridor ahead. He skidded to a halt, straining to hear the girl's footsteps. But there was nothing.

Nothing except a rasping electronic voice that said: 'Up a bit your end, Bott.'

'If you say so, Bill.'

'I do, Bott. Whoa – that's enough. Maybe too much, take it down a bit.'

The two robots were fixing a picture to the wall of the corridor. Each was holding one end of the large painting as they struggled to get it level. The Doctor stuffed his hands in his jacket pockets and wandered over to them. There were several doors off the corridor, and as he passed each he tried the handle. They were all locked.

'Want me to take a look and tell you when it's level?' he asked.

'If you would,' Bill said.

'Be a great help,' Bott agreed.

'Do you believe in ghosts?' the Doctor asked as he held the picture steady so Bill could fix it in place with a glue-gun attached to one of his spindly arms.

'Depends what you mean by ghosts,' Bott said.

'Do you?' Bill asked the Doctor.

'I'm not sure,' the Doctor admitted. 'But I don't think so. Not, you know, clanking chains and wailing grey ladies and all that. But imprints of the past. Personal demons...'

'Bits of memory storage that become detached and float about interrupting other thought processes,' Bott suggested.

'Or a little girl called Janna,' the Doctor said quietly.

'Ah.' Bill nodded.

'Oh.' Bott took a step backwards.

'Who must have come this way,' the Doctor said.

'I expect,' Bill said slowly, 'that she knows all the secret hidey holes and hidden passages and nooks and crannies in Castle Extremis.'

'She's certainly not a ghost,' Bott said. 'Though,' he went on in an unnecessarily loud voice, 'I can't say I've seen her recently.'

'She didn't come past here,' Bill agreed, pointing at his own feet. As he finished speaking the Doctor was sure he heard a giggle from somewhere nearby.

'Er, pardon,' Bott said, metallic clawed hand over his speaker grille.

'Robots,' the Doctor told him, 'do not burp.'

'You sure?' Bill asked.

'Look,' the Doctor went on quickly, 'she's not in trouble. Though there's certainly trouble to be had. Bags of it. Sack fulls. Or should that be sacks full? Whatever – anyway, I don't think she killed anyone.'

'What?' Bill exclaimed.

'Who didn't she kill?' Bott asked.

'Well, First Secretary Chekz for starters. At least, I hope it isn't for starters. But I'm afraid it might be.'

'Janna killed Chekz?' Bill said. The disbelief was obvious even in the electronic speech.

'No, no, no,' the Doctor said. 'That's what she *didn't* do. Someone did, but not Janna. I mean, why would she, even if she could? Well, maybe there's loads of reasons but I won't know till I talk to her. So I need to talk to her.'

'Because she didn't kill Chekz,' Bott said slowly, as if wanting to be sure he had this right.

'She might have seen who did,' the Doctor said. 'And if that's the case, then Janna is in danger.'

The two robots looked at each other for several moments. Then Bill said: 'Janna, I think you need to talk to the Doctor.'

'And,' Bott said, 'the Doctor needs to talk to you.'

What had looked like a solid section of the wall swung slowly open. A door. Beyond it, the Doctor could see the little fair-haired girl standing there. Her eyes narrowed as she assessed him. Behind her, through the door, was a small room lit by one of the flickering electric firebrands attached to the wall. There was a huddle of blankets that might have been a bed, and little chair beside a plain wooden table. Not much of a home, the Doctor thought.

'Come in,' Janna said. 'You'll have to sit on the floor.'

The negotiations had been adjourned for several hours. The guides were all confined to the servants' quarters – which, judging by the reactions Martha saw, was hardly an inconvenience. Two of the guards carried the body away, and Defron said he would arrange for Bill and Bott to clean the floor. Martha could imagine they'd be less than happy about it.

'Thank goodness the press haven't arrived yet,' Defron said as he watched the body of Chekz being carried away under a blanket.

'Usually he's complaining they haven't been allowed in to cover the proceedings yet,' Stellman said quietly to Martha.

'The guards have weapons,' Martha said. They had guns slung over their backs as they carried the body away, leaving Martha and Stellman standing alone outside the locked door to the Zerugians' quarters.

'So?'

'You said there were weapons detectors.'

'The guards are neutral. There's always a chance someone will try to attack the conference, but they're here for show more than anything. They are unable to intervene in anything relating directly to the negotiations, or in any trouble between Anthium and Zerugma, without a direct order from an official GA representative.'

'Yeah, but they have got guns. Why stab Chekz rather than take one of the guns and do it?'

'Oh I see.' Stellman looked at Martha, his expression giving away nothing of his thoughts. 'Each weapon is bio-coded to the guard who was issued with it. Without that guard's hand on the barrel, their finger on the trigger – without detecting their DNA and sweat and the exact rhythm of their heartbeat, the gun won't fire. Even if it's been released for use, and of course that won't happen without official GA codes.'

Martha guessed she was probably expected to know all that. 'So, obviously it was not one of the guards who killed Chekz, then.'

'If they'd shot him, if the weapon was released for use and then actually used, we'd know who it was from the signature of the bullet. Trace it back to the gun, and the gun to the bio-code. If one of the guards decided to kill Chekz, they wouldn't shoot him unless they wanted to get caught.'

'Oh,' Martha said, disappointed. 'So it really could have been anyone.'

Stellman nodded. 'Yes. It really could.'

'And you're an assassin.'

He smiled. 'Used to be. During the war. When we were fighting. I was responsible for Special Measures against the Zerugians. That covered all manner of covert operations, including assassination if necessary.'

Martha shook her head. 'How could you do that?'

Stellman didn't react to her disgust. 'We were at war. It was my job. I was good at it.'

Martha sensed that there wasn't anything more to say. 'Excuse me,' she said. 'I think I'll go and rest in my room. It's all been a bit of a shock.'

'I'll see you later then.'

Stellman nodded and started slowly along the corridor in the direction of the negotiating chamber. Martha set off in the other direction, hoping it was the way to the rooms she and the Doctor had been allocated. Not that it mattered too much if it wasn't. She reached the end of the passage and turned out of sight.

She counted slowly to ten before she turned again, and looked back down the passage towards the Zerugians' quarters.

Stellman was standing there. He must have waited till Martha was gone, then returned. She watched as the man fiddled with the lock, and the door swung open. Martha ducked quickly out of sight as Stellman turned, checking he was alone.

She looked back in time to see Stellman step into the Zerugians' rooms, and close the door quietly behind him.

'Is this your home?' the Doctor asked, looking round the cramped space.

'The whole castle is my home, silly.' Janna was sitting

cross-legged on the makeshift bed, holding one of the blankets in a bundle in front of her.

'Of course. Silly me. Cosy here, though, isn't it? Like a den. I've always wanted a den.'

Janna smiled. 'I've got loads of rooms. All over the place. Lots of dens. Got anything to eat?'

This caught the Doctor by surprise. 'Er, sorry.' He patted his pockets. 'Don't think I have, actually. Can I ask you something? It is important.'

'About the murder?'

'Well, yes.'

'I didn't do it,' Janna assured him seriously.

'I know.'

'Then what?'

'I wondered if you knew who did?' the Doctor said. 'If you saw anything?'

She shook her head and hugged the blanket to her tight.

'It's all right. You're not in trouble or anything.'

She turned away. 'Didn't see nothing.'

The Doctor sat next to her on the thin mattress that was lying on the floor. 'But you do know. You know something. Tell me, please. I can help. I'm good at helping. I can help you if you'll let me.'

'Don't need help,' she said into the blanket.

'That's good. I'd best be going then. Toddling along, pushing off, making a move.'

The Doctor stood by the door, looking back at the little girl on the bed. Her cheeks were stained with silent tears, their trails catching the flickering light. 'What are you afraid of?' the Doctor asked gently.

Her eyes met his, just for an instant. 'The man in the mirror.' Then she looked away. 'And my sister.'

'Your sister is dead,' the Doctor told her. 'I'm sorry, I really am. But that's the way it is. She's gone.'

'I know.' Janna flopped back on the bed and pulled the blanket up to her chin, gripping it tight. 'But why's she come back?'

From the other side of the door, Martha could hear the faint sounds of drawers and cupboards being opened and shut. Stellman was searching the room – but for what? She briefly considered knocking on the door and simply asking him.

'*Such* a bad idea,' she muttered. And she had a far better one. If Stellman was busy searching the Zerugians' rooms – and God help him if Orlo came back – then Stellman's own quarters would be empty.

She passed Bill and Bott fixing paintings to a wall in a passageway, and asked them if they knew where Stellman's room was.

'We know where everyone's rooms are,' Bill assured her.

'Everyone,' Bott agreed. 'Lady Casaubon's along there, General Orlo and Secretary Chekz share a suite back that way.'

'I know,' Martha said. 'And Stellman?'

'It's a nice suite, actually,' Bill told her. 'Shared

conference room and kitchens, though they don't cook much. Then state rooms and bedrooms. En suite, you know.'

'Yes, lovely I'm sure. Stellman?'

'I think Chekz likes to make cocoa,' Bott said after a moment's thought.

'Not any more,' Bill pointed out. 'Then there's Professor Thorodin. He doesn't slum it down here with the delegates, he has—'

'Where is Stellman's room?' Martha asked again in exasperation. 'That's all I want to know. It isn't much, just a simple question.'

'You want to know where Stellman's room is?' Bott said.

Martha nodded, not trusting herself to speak.

'Why didn't you say? It's along there, past the intersection then second on the right,' Bill told her.

'Thank you.'

'But he's not there,' Bott called after her as Martha set off down the passageway.

'And the door's locked,' Bill put in.

'I'll manage,' Martha told them, then wondered if she should have said that. No, they wouldn't guess what she was up to. She'd be quite safe.

'If you give it a good thump, just below the keyhole,' Bill shouted loudly after her, 'you'll find the lock springs open. Been meaning to fix it.'

'It's down for next week,' Bott was saying as Martha covered her ears and ran.

'Not interested. Not listening,' she said.

'You sure it's next week?' Bill was asking.

But Martha had gone.

A moment later, part of the wall of the passage swung open and the Doctor stepped out. He smiled at Bill and Bott, tapped his index finger against his front teeth, and set off along the passageway.

'Your friend went the other way,' Bill said.

The Doctor wasn't really listening. 'That's nice,' he said, continuing along the corridor. He was going back over what Janna had said and wondering how much of a grip on reality the poor girl had.

He turned a corner and almost bumped into a figure coming the other way. 'Oh, hi there,' he said. 'You seen Martha?'

'She went that way,' Stellman said, pointing in the direction the Doctor was heading.

'Thanks.' The Doctor continued on his way, and Stellman continued on his. Back to his room.

At the sound of the key in the lock, Martha froze. She had only just got inside Stellman's rooms. He had a suite that included a study, a kitchen and a bedroom. She'd not even checked his desk.

Hiding places were few and far between. Heavy drapes hung beside a large oval window that looked out onto the floodlit gardens. Martha hurried behind them, burying herself in the folds of material. In the glass of the window, she could see the reflection of Stellman as he came into the room.

He looked at the key, as if puzzled. His other hand was still in his jacket pocket. Martha was not sure she'd ever seen it come out of his pocket. Perhaps he didn't have a hand – like Napoleon. Or was it Nelson?

Stellman put the key down on a table and walked through to the kitchen. She could hear water running – maybe he was getting a drink. Yes, she was sure it was Nelson.

While Stellman was out of sight, Martha crept from behind the curtain and tip-toed to the door, which was still standing slightly open. She could be out of here before he came back. No problem.

'What are you doing in here?'

Martha froze again. Stellman was standing behind her. Watching her. His hand still thrust into his jacket pocket. Problem.

'I was...' Martha's voice dried in her throat. She tried again. 'I thought you'd come back to your room. I was looking for you. The door was open.'

Stellman hesitated and, though his expression was as blank and unreadable as ever, for a moment she thought she was all right. But then he said: 'No, it wasn't. The lock's not terribly effective, I know, but it works well enough.'

'You were searching Chekz's room,' Martha accused.

'Yes, I was. But it's not me that needs the excuse just now, is it?'

'And why not?'

By way of answer he pulled his hand from his pocket. Martha gasped, realising. All the time, whenever he had spoken to her, to the Doctor, to anyone, Stellman had been pointing a gun at them. A gun hidden in his pocket.

A transparent gun, the mechanism and the bullets clearly visible within.

'The weapons detectors don't scan for glass,' Martha realised.

And Stellman smiled.

Someone was following him. The Doctor could hear footsteps echoing his own. They were being careful. It wasn't Janna – the footfalls were too heavy. And she didn't seem to care who knew she was watching them anyway.

The Doctor still hadn't caught up with Martha. He'd looked in her room, but she wasn't there. She wasn't in his room either, he'd checked there too. His next stop was the Great Hall en route to the negotiating chamber.

Just before he reached the hall, he ducked quickly into an alcove. The footsteps behind him hesitated. There was a pause. Then they resumed – quicker. Whoever it was must be afraid they'd lost him. The Doctor pressed back into the alcove and let the cloaked figure walk quickly past.

Then he stepped out into the light, and called after it: 'You looking for me?'

The monk stopped and turned. The hood of the cloak hid the figure's face.

'I know you can't speak while you're wearing that, but I do have a few questions.' The Doctor walked slowly towards the monk. 'Because you've been following me, haven't you? We can do this sort of multiple choice if you like. That way you won't have to break any rules or actually say anything.'

The hood of the cloak moved slightly. The voice that came from within was old, rasping, barely more than a whisper. 'You have the book.'

The Doctor stopped. 'Book?'

'I saw you find it.'

'Ah, yes, the book.' He took the glass book from his pocket. 'This, you mean?'

'Read it,' the monk hissed.

'Yeah, well, bit of a problem there. You see—'

'Read it, Doctor!'

'I would, if I could. But it's in some sort of code.'

'Mirror writing.'

'Of course.' The Doctor slapped his forehead with his free hand. 'How could I be so stupid. Mirror writing.' He held the book open for the monk to see. 'Only it isn't, is it? I'd spot mirror writing a mile off. Taught Leonardo how to do it. Left-handed as well. Think I don't know mirror writing? This is *not* mirror writing.'

The monk gave a low chuckle. 'Nevertheless, you can read it in the mirror.'

'The mirror? You mean *the* mirror? A particular

mirror? What is it then, a symmetrical transformation keyed to the refractive index of both types of glass or something?'

'Does it matter?'

'Matter?' The Doctor laughed. 'Of course it matters. If that's how it's done, then it's brilliant. Genius.' He stared down at the open page of thin glass. 'But how would you encode it in the first place?'

There was no answer. The Doctor looked up, and saw that he was alone. The monk had gone.

'Not much of a conversationalist,' the Doctor muttered. He was already hurrying to the Great Hall. There was only one mirror in the castle he knew of that could reasonably be called *the* mirror. The Mortal Mirror in the Great Hall.

The huge room was empty. The Doctor walked towards the mirror, holding the glass book open in front of him at the first page. As soon as he was close enough to make out the reflection clearly, he stopped.

'Oh that is just so clever,' he breathed.

The meaningless symbols on the glass reflected back as letters – as words, sentences.

'I am the Man in the Mirror,' the first line read. 'And this is my story.'

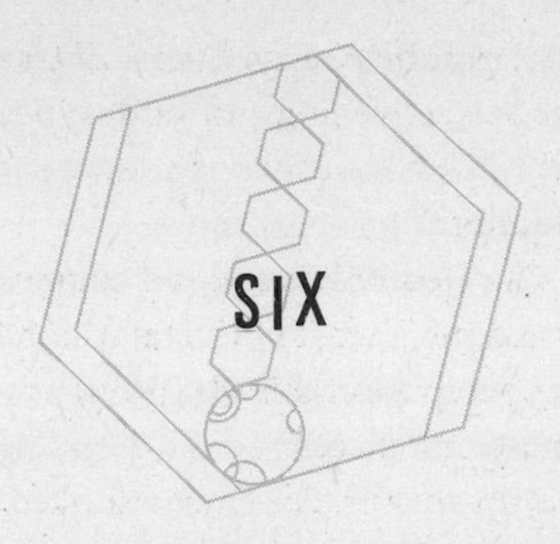

SIX

Martha didn't hesitate. If she gave herself time to think, she knew, she would just stand there and wait for Stellman to shoot her. He was a professional assassin – he'd told her that. No way could he miss. And Stellman knew that Martha was aware of that.

So she hoped she had surprise on her side as she dived for the door.

She expected to hear the crack of a shot, to feel the stab of pain as the bullet caught her. But there was nothing. Martha was out of the room, struggling to her feet and running down the corridor.

Behind her, she heard a door slam. Heavy, rapid footsteps. He was coming after her. Surprise was gone now, and as soon as he got a clear shot…

Round the corner. How fast was Stellman? He looked fit, but was he quick? Breaths coming in gasps, heart thumping. Stopping to try a door – locked. Running again.

'In a hurry?' Bill asked as Martha sprinted towards the two robots still putting up pictures.

'He's got – a – gun!' Martha gasped as she approached. 'Help me!'

'Don't like guns,' Bott said. 'Best to hide.'

'My defensive mode burned out years ago,' Bill said sadly.

'Hide where? Can't you slow him down?' She was level with Bott now. 'Buy me time to get away?'

Bott's round head tilted slightly. 'And get shot? You're joking.'

'I am not joking. Thanks for nothing.' Martha ran on.

Further down the corridor, Bill was holding open a section of wall. 'In here,' he hissed in an electronic whisper. Then he looked through the door and added: 'Sorry Janna.'

Martha didn't wait to ask why a part of the wall had opened, or how, or where it led. She ran inside and collapsed gasping on the floor.

The wall closed behind her. The light faded to a flickering gloom. Martha sat up and looked round, her breath still ragged and painful.

On the other side of the small hidden room was a thin mattress with a pile of blankets bundled on top of it. Beside the pile of blankets sat a pale, fair-haired girl.

'You're funny,' Janna said.

***

The book was a diary. An account of the man's life, or at least a part of it. The man in the mirror. Suddenly a lot of things were becoming clearer, and not just the unintelligible symbols on the cold, brittle, glass pages.

It was just getting even more interesting, when Defron arrived. The Doctor could see him reflected in the mirror, standing in the doorway, as if uncertain whether to come in.

'You seen Martha?' the Doctor called. 'I thought she came this way.' He closed the diary and put it back in his jacket pocket.

'No,' Defron said. 'No, I haven't.' He walked slowly towards the Doctor. 'Could I have a word?'

'Any word you like. *Meringue* is a good one. Or *cropper*. You know – as in *come a cropper*.'

Defron did not seem amused. 'I sent a report to the Galactic Alliance,' he said. 'Telling them about the... incident.'

'Fair enough.' The Doctor nodded. Then he realised what this might mean. 'Ah. You mentioned me and Martha?'

'I did, yes. As we already have GA observers here, I suggested that further intervention by the justice authorities was not necessary.'

'And they told you that they'd never heard of us?' The Doctor shook his head sadly.

'They will admit to having two Special Agents on site, as well as Colonel Blench's peacekeeping force. Though the troops have rather limited powers, of course. But when I mentioned that I had already made contact with you…' He opened his hands in a silent apology.

'We get this a lot,' the Doctor confided, looking round as if to check they were alone. 'Becomes a bit of a bore, to be honest. But what can you do? I'm sure I can rely on your discretion. Bloke like you – you understand how it works.'

'Er,' Defron said.

'I mean, Martha Mouse and Doctor Duck? Is that the best aliases they could come up with? I ask you. I despair sometimes, I really do.'

'Er,' said Defron again. 'Quite.'

'Still,' the Doctor went on, 'that's what happens when you get involved in covert operations.'

'*Covert?*' Defron's eyes widened in something close to panic.

'Well, clandestine anyway. Well, undercover. Well – you know, we have to be discreet, you can see that.'

'Yes,' Defron said, but he sounded dubious.

'And I know we can rely on you. Told the General Secretary before we came, actually.'

'Really?'

'Oh yes. Teddy, I said…'

Defron frowned. 'Her name is Canasta. Canasta Ventron.'

'Well, obviously. But I call her Teddy. Always have. Ever since we were at school together.'

'She's in her eighties.'

'Didn't you know she used to be a teacher? Well, you

live and learn. Anyway, Teddy, I said – Defron's a good man. A pragmatist. A *realist*. He'll understand the need for caution, for playing it close, for going undercover. And as long as everyone else believes we're just GA observers and no more than that, then I'm happy for Defron to know the truth. He'll be glad to help in any way he can.'

'I'm sorry,' Defron said, still looking confused. 'I had no idea. So – who exactly are you really?'

The Doctor tapped his nose. 'Need to know,' he whispered conspiratorially. 'The less you know, the less you can divulge.'

'I've sent the guides to their rooms for the duration, and I've assigned guards to be with Lady Casaubon and General Orlo at all times. Orlo wasn't pleased by that, I can tell you. But, do you really think there's still danger?'

'Chekz is dead.'

'Someone wants to start another war between Zerugma and Anthium?'

'Chekz is dead,' the Doctor said again. 'It might be an incident, but it wasn't an accident.'

Defron nodded. He was looking pale. He sank down into one of the upright wooden chairs at the side of the room. 'How can I help, Doctor? Er – or is it...?'

'Doctor will do for now. And you can help by telling me something. Something that may be vitally important, however trivial it might seem to you.'

'Yes?'

The Doctor leaned close. 'Who,' he asked, 'was Manfred Grieg?'

Martha put her finger to her lips. With her ear pressed to the stone door, she could just make out voices from the other side of the wall.

'She did come this way,' Bill was saying.

'Kept going. Went past me,' Bott explained. 'Going that way.'

'Did you see where she went at the end?' Stellman's voice demanded.

'At the end?' Bill asked.

Could robots lie, Martha wondered? And if they could, would they? They had hidden her in this secret room with Janna. Or had they trapped her in there and made it easier for Stellman?

'No, didn't see her get to the end,' Bill said. 'Did you, Bott?'

'I did not, Bill.'

'Then, maybe…' Stellman's voice sounded closer now. There was a scraping on the other side of the stone. 'I wonder…' Had he seen the outline of the hidden door?

'Left,' Bott announced suddenly.

'What?' The scraping stopped.

'There's a good chance she went left.'

'But you didn't see her go left.'

'That's true,' Bott agreed.

'But we didn't see her go right either,' Bill explained. 'So there's a good chance she didn't.'

'If you see her,' Stellman said with what sounded like great control, 'please tell her that I'd like a word.'

'No problem,' Bill said.

'It'll be our pleasure,' Bott agreed.

'Everyone knows the story,' Defron said. 'The story of Manfred Grieg and the Mortal Mirror. But you'd do better to ask Professor Thorodin. He's the expert.'

'Oh.' The Doctor sounded disappointed. 'I'd much rather ask you. I mean, he's so boring. But you're a diplomat, an orator. You make language come alive. You really do.'

'That's very kind of you.' Defron cleared his throat. 'Well, er, as you know, Manfred Grieg was Chief Minister to Kendal Pennard.'

'Who was, of course...?' the Doctor prompted.

'Who was of course Lord High Advocate for Anthium and the Governor of Castle Extremis.'

'As we both well know,' the Doctor's agreed quickly.

'And it was Grieg, by all accounts, who advised Pennard on the strategy used to recapture Extremis after the Second Occupation, a little over a hundred years ago. Quite brilliant. Really, quite, quite brilliant.'

'Oh, I like brilliant,' the Doctor agreed.

'Anyway, by way of thanks, Pennard gave Grieg a mirror. The Mortal Mirror.' He pointed down the Great Hall to where the replica was hanging. 'And I imagine Grieg was suitably impressed and grateful.'

'I'm sure he was. Go on.'

'But what he didn't know was that Pennard had tricked him. He was jealous of Grieg's brilliance, and was afraid his minister would supplant him, though there is no evidence to suggest that Grieg was especially ambitious. Though, I suppose...' Defron considered for a moment before going on. 'Well, he was a politician.'

'Yeah, right.' The Doctor laughed. 'And whoever heard of a politician who wasn't cunning and conniving and ambitious, eh?' He caught Defron's eye, and his grin faded. 'Sorry. Joke. Go on.'

'The Mortal Mirror was made for Pennard by the Darksmiths of Karagula.'

The Doctor whistled. 'They knew a thing or two. Must have cost him a packet and a half. Maybe two packets and a half.'

'Perhaps. But what Manfred Grieg did not know was that the mirror was a trap. It was hung here, just as the replica that General Orlo has so kindly provided hangs now. There was a great feast to celebrate the victory and to honour Grieg. Or so he thought.'

'That's always ominous – the "so he thought" bit.' The Doctor shivered. 'Gets me every time. So, big feast, mirror unveiled, huge surprise for Grieg, yes?'

Defron nodded. 'He thought he was being honoured. Instead Pennard denounced him as a traitor and claimed that he had tried to sell the Anthium forces out to Zerugma. Soldiers rushed in, and Grieg backed away. But there was nowhere for him to go.'

'Except,' the Doctor said thoughtfully, 'into the mirror.'

'So the legend says. The Mortal Mirror, when primed and adjusted in a certain way, reflects not this world, but rather an image of another identical world. A dark realm beyond our own where time and space are inverted and...' Defron shook his head. 'I forget the rest, but you get the idea.'

The Doctor was still staring at the mirror. 'I do indeed. The Darksmiths had the power to reshape the stuff of the universe. They could open portals into other worlds, or so it was said. Didn't know they went in for mirrors.'

He leaned forward and tapped the glass gently. Then he breathed heavily on it, and wiped away the misty condensation with the back of his hand.

'So Pennard tricked Grieg into the mirror world and trapped him there,' he went on. 'Which seems a bit convoluted. There must have been more to it than that, or he'd have just had the man shot. But whyever he did it, Pennard then disconnected or unplugged or switched off whatever mechanism opened the portal, and that was it. Grieg became the man in the mirror.'

'And the mirror became... just a mirror,' said Defron.

'Until it was destroyed by the Zerugians,' the Doctor said.

Defron nodded. 'They feared that Grieg might one day escape, and they knew better than Pennard that he was the one man who could defeat them and overthrow the Third Occupation.'

'So this mirror is just a copy,' the Doctor said quietly.

'That's right. It's only a story. And this is just an ordinary mirror.'

'Just an ordinary mirror,' the Doctor murmured. 'That can translate Manfred Grieg's glass diary.'

Janna was watching her with curiosity as Martha pressed her ear to the stone. She couldn't hear anything now, and hoped that Stellman had moved off. She'd give it a few more minutes, she decided, before taking a look. Just in case…

'You hiding?' Janna asked.

'Just a bit.'

'I hide. This is my hidey hole.'

'Sorry. But there was this man with a gun.'

'The guards have guns,' Janna said dismissively. 'But they don't work. It's all right. I don't mind you being here. You can visit. Like your friend.'

Martha turned in surprise. 'The Doctor was here?'

'A few minutes ago. He's funny too.'

'You're telling me. So, is this where you live?'

'One of the places. I got lots of homes.'

'And how do you live? I mean, where do you get food and stuff?'

Janna looked at Martha like she was mad. 'Kitchens of course. Where does your food come from?'

'You just take it?'

'If I have to. But they know me. They give me stuff. I used to work in the kitchens sometimes,' she said. Then she looked away. 'With my sister. Not any more.'

'I heard about your sister,' Martha said gently. 'I'm sorry.' She wondered if she should go and sit by the girl. Give her a hug. Or would that just freak the poor girl out?

'Sorry she's gone?' Janna asked. 'Or sorry she's come back?'

Martha nodded slowly, remembering what Gonfer had told them about the girl's sudden changes of mood. 'I think maybe I met your sister. In the courtyard.'

Janna sighed. 'That was me.'

'She was rude. Abrupt.'

'Yeah. I get like that. Sorry.'

'Is that what happens?' Now Martha did go and sit beside the girl. 'Does she sort of, I don't know, take you over? Do you feel like you're her?'

Janna edged along the mattress away from Martha. 'Are you crazy?' Her eyes widened. 'Do you think I'm crazy?'

'No, of course not.'

'She died. In the gardens. Gonfer found her, all...' The girl shook her head, her eyes moist in the flickering light. 'All dead. He saw what happened. Now he's so nice and kind and he gets me food.'

'That's good,' Martha said. She wasn't sure what else she could say. She took Janna's hand, and was relieved the girl did not pull away again.

'Why does he do that?' Janna wailed suddenly, turning to Martha. She wiped away her tears with the back of her free hand. 'Why is he so nice? I used to tease him, and upset him. I was horrid to him and now he's so good to me. Why?'

'Perhaps he feels sorry for you.' Martha could feel her own tears welling up.

'He used to get so angry.' Janna shook her head. 'My sister was nice to him and I was horrid. Now he's nice to me. And she's back.'

'What do you mean, she's back?'

'I mean she's here in the castle. She follows me. I see her watching from the shadows. I hear her footsteps behind me. I go to my secret places – like here – and I find she's been there already. I've got places no one else knows about, not even Bill and Bott, and she goes there and moves things. Lives there.' She looked at Martha, eyes wide and lips trembling. 'How can she *live* there, when she's *dead*?'

Martha could only shake her head. It would do no good to tell the girl she was imagining things. And what if she wasn't? What if she really was being haunted by her own dead sister?

But Martha did not have to answer. Because at that moment the hidden door to the corridor outside swung open.

Stellman was standing framed in the opening, one hand in his jacket pocket.

'I'm sorry it took me so long to get the door open,' he said.

'How did you find us?' Janna demanded.

'Bill and Bott.'

'So,' Martha said, 'robots can't lie.'

'Oh yes they can,' Stellman said. 'It's just that they're not very good at it.'

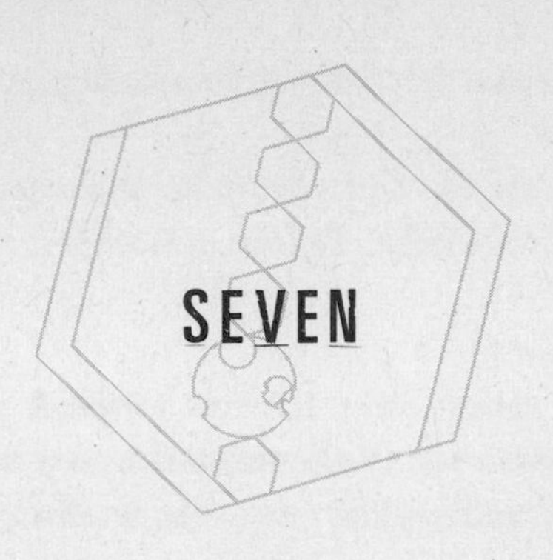

SEVEN

He had watched the Doctor. Watched the way he looked at the mirror and the way he reacted to Defron's account of the story of Manfred Grieg. The way he examined the glass book… And he was worried. This Doctor could be trouble. It was best to take no chances.

He waited until Defron and the Doctor headed back to the negotiating chamber, then slipped into the Great Hall. There was no one else there, so he didn't need to worry about the angles. Didn't need to avoid the mirror.

Nursing his shattered arm, he fumbled with the hidden mechanism. He reached round the wooden frame, pulling it slightly away from the wall, feeling for the controls. They were stiff with age but he knew what to do. He had to hold the mirror away from the wall with his broken wrist while he set the mechanism.

***

The Doctor was head down, hands deep in pockets as they walked.

'It's too late for Zerugma to send a replacement for First Secretary Chekz,' Defron was saying. 'Even if they wanted to.'

'You reckon?'

'There's always been tension between the military and the politicians. Chekz was billed as a compromise. A politician with military experience, albeit a long time ago.'

'So the politicians won,' the Doctor mused. 'Not necessarily a bad thing.'

'Not a bad thing at all,' Defron agreed. 'The military was furious and insisted on sending General Orlo as his aide.'

'Because he's a hardliner?'

'Absolutely.'

The Doctor nodded. 'And with the death of Chekz, they'll see Orlo as the best choice anyway. Uncompromising, determined, firm and resolute. With the moral high ground now as well.'

'Don't forget bloodthirsty,' Defron said in a lowered voice.

'Oh?'

'He led the Zerugian troops into Mendalla. And we all know what happened there.'

They were almost at the negotiating chamber.

'Yeah,' the Doctor said. 'Yeah, that was… nasty. OK, so we add bloodthirsty to our list. Still leaves a great big question though. A huge glaring whopping humdinger of a question.'

The soldiers either side of the door snapped to attention.

'Which is?' Defron asked as they paused outside the room.

'Why did he offer the replica of the Mortal Mirror?'

'A goodwill gesture, he said.'

'Except, we just decided he doesn't have any goodwill. So what do you reckon – is the leopard changing his spots? Or will there be crocodile tears before bedtime?'

There was a hushed silence in the room, the stillness of shock and grief. A soldier now stood immediately behind Orlo, another behind Lady Casaubon.

'Anyone seen Martha?' the Doctor asked as he sat down. Lady Casaubon shook her head. General Orlo sat still and impassive. 'No?'

Defron took his place at the head of the curved table. 'And where's Stellman?' he asked.

The little girl was shaking with anger. 'Don't you dare shoot my friend,' she told Stellman.

'I wouldn't dream of it,' Stellman told her. He held his hands open and empty for her to see.

'He *did* have a gun,' Martha said warily.

'Yes, I did. But I wasn't going to shoot you.'

'Oh, excuse me? You were just waving it about to look cool were you? You aren't supposed to have guns here. You know that – you told me that.'

'You really think that Orlo doesn't have some way of protecting himself?'

'Well, Chekz didn't,' Martha shot back.

'All the more reason for me to be able to defend Lady Casaubon.'

'And yourself.'

'True,' he admitted. 'Though on the grand scale of things I am very unimportant.' He sounded like he meant it.

'I want you both to go away now,' Janna said. 'I don't like you,' she told Stellman. 'You're rude and bossy.'

'Probably,' he admitted. 'I'm sorry. I shall be happy to leave. I was looking for Martha. Now I have found her.'

'Don't you hurt her,' Janna warned again.

Stellman stepped back out into the corridor. 'Shall we?' He gestured for Martha to join him.

Martha said a quick goodbye to Janna, then hurried after Stellman. 'So, why did you chase after me, then?' she demanded. The door in the corridor wall slammed shut behind her.

'You saw I had a gun. I don't want Orlo or Defron to know that. Or Lady Casaubon,' he added. 'She would disapprove.'

'I bet. So that's it? Just wanted to ask me to keep my trap shut?'

'And to ask you why you were in my room.'

'I told you, I went to find you...'

Stellman cut her off. 'I didn't believe you then and I don't now.'

They were walking as they talked. Martha realised they were heading back towards Stellman's room. Was that a good idea? She wasn't convinced by his excuses for chasing after her, though on reflection they did make sense.

As if to convince her, he said: 'So, can I rely on your discretion?'

'For now,' Martha decided. 'But what were you doing in Chekz's rooms?'

'The same as you were in mine, I imagine. Searching.'

'What for?'

He shrugged. 'I didn't really know. Some clue as to who killed Chekz, and why. It wasn't me, you know,' he added.

'You are an assassin,' Martha pointed out.

'True. But everyone is aware of that. It's the killer no one knows about who is most dangerous. And a more likely suspect.'

'So did you find anything? Any clues to who this unknown killer might be?'

'I did. But…'

'But what?'

'Well, I don't really know what to make of it.'

Martha frowned. 'Why – what is it?'

'I will show you. It's in my room.'

Janna knew her sister was watching her. Following her. 'Go away,' she shouted back down the corridor. 'You're dead – go away and leave me alone!'

But when she turned and ran on, she could hear her sister's laughter echoing after her.

'Going to hide,' Janna said to herself. 'Going to hide and never come out. Then you'll have to go away.'

There were voices coming the other way, but Janna didn't care. She turned down a side passage and cut past the kitchens. She'd go to the Great Hall and hide there. She didn't like it so much now, didn't feel so safe as she used to – not since...

But she hoped her sister wouldn't find her there. They weren't allowed in the Great Hall. It was out of bounds. And her sister was a good girl, always obeyed the rules.

When she was alive.

'It was under the side table by the door. I think it got chipped when it fell.'

Martha took it from Stellman. It was surprisingly heavy. 'It looks so real. It's... unnerving isn't it?'

'Exquisite,' he said. 'Or grotesque. I'm really not sure which.'

It was a hand. The wrist was a shattered broken mess, and the end of a finger had snapped off. There were several chips out of it – where the material showed through the paint. If it was paint.

'It's so realistic,' Martha said. 'If it wasn't damaged, you'd think it was real. It must have been cast or something, I suppose. You think the murderer left it?'

'Dropped it maybe. Or perhaps he broke it off whatever he used to stab Chekz.'

'Like an arm?' Martha suggested.

'Who can say.' Stellman held the broken hand up and the chipped facets and the stub of the wrist caught and reflected the light. 'But it *is* made of glass.'

There were various formalities that Defron insisted would have to be sorted out. They were boring procedural things like awaiting the official ratification of General Orlo as the new chief negotiator, and that would have to come from Zerugma.

Lady Casaubon and Defron were both agreed that, so long as they noted that these things needed to be addressed, they could continue to negotiate in good faith. But Orlo insisted that they adjourn discussions until every 't' was crossed and every 'i' dotted.

'So long as we avoid crossed eyes,' the Doctor said brightly. Leaving them to it, he headed off to Martha's quarters to see if she'd turned up there. She had not.

On his way back to the Great Hall to continue reading the glass diary, the Doctor nodded pleasantly to a GA soldier and gave another the thumbs-up. He made his way along the deserted passageway leading to the Great Hall, and encountered Lady Casaubon emerging from the negotiations.

'Tell me,' he said, 'if there's no one here but us and the soldiers, why were the guides still dressing up and wandering about until Defron confined them to barracks?'

Lady Casaubon laughed. 'Defron suggested they be

sent away, given a holiday or whatever. Obviously the castle had to be closed to visitors for the duration of the negotiations. Anyway, the Union objected. Said he was denying them their livelihood.'

'But while it's closed, there's no one to guide,' the Doctor said. 'So why bother? Why weren't they all sitting round playing Monopoly?'

'Because Defron told the Union that if they were still being employed then they had to work their usual shifts and he'd be checking and would dismiss any who didn't.'

The Doctor grinned. 'Really? He's good at this diplomacy thing, isn't he? Didn't the Union object to that?'

'Of course. But Defron also said he would hear reasoned argument only from the guides themselves. And only while they were officially on duty in that capacity, not when they were merely private citizens between shifts.'

The Doctor's grin widened. 'And when they're on duty the guides aren't allowed to talk.'

'One of them sent him a short note,' Lady Casaubon said. 'Defron asked him if he could clarify certain aspects of it, either verbally or in writing. One hundred and five of them.'

'And did he?'

'What do you think?'

'I think Martha would have done. Maybe she's helping him with it now. I haven't seen her for a while.

She's always wandering off,' the Doctor said. 'Your Mr Stellman got the same problem, has he?'

'Not usually. He is most attentive, so I can only imagine he is detained by some matter of importance. Or which he believes is important.'

'You don't share his priorities?' the Doctor wondered.

'Oh, at my age you appreciate there is very little that is truly important.'

'You're telling me,' the Doctor said. 'But Martha's important. Ah, yes – should have thought of that,' he went on as two familiar figures turned into the corridor ahead of them, just past the Great Hall. Martha and Stellman, together.

'Doctor!' Martha called, hurrying up to him. Where have you been?'

'Where have *I* been?'

'Stellman's found something. I think it may be—'

'Important? Could be. What is it?' He turned to Stellman. 'Show me, show me. What have you got? Fingerprint found at the scene? An unusual-looking stone? Recipe for Banana Surprise?'

'Banana Surprise?' Lady Casaubon said.

'Yes, it's great.' Miming the actions, the Doctor explained: 'You get a banana, right? Carefully peel it, and take out the banana. Then stuff the skin with cotton wool and sew it back up again.'

'And that's a Banana Surprise?' Martha said.

'It is for whoever tries to eat the banana. I like

bananas.' He was looking over Martha's shoulder as he spoke. He was watching Janna slip quietly along the passageway and into the Great Hall. 'There's that little girl...' he said.

As he spoke, Janna's head appeared back round the doorway. She put her finger to her lips then disappeared again.

'There's that little girl,' the Doctor said quickly, 'who said "I know how to spell banana, but I don't know when to stop." Love that story.' He grinned. 'Never know when to stop telling it though. Sorry, what were we talking about?'

'Bananas, apparently,' Martha said.

'Before that?'

Stellman held something out to them. 'This.'

The Doctor took it. 'A glass hand.' He weighed it in his palm. He pretended to shake it in greeting. He examined it closely. 'Yep, definitely glass. Where did you get it? Second hand shop?'

'Someone left it in Chekz's room,' Martha said.

'Really? Careless of them.' He gave it back to Stellman. 'Unhand me, sir. Here you go.'

'You think it is not important?' Lady Casaubon asked.

'When you get to my age...' the Doctor told her. 'Who knows. Maybe. But it's part of a puzzle and we need more of the pieces before we can see where it fits, before we can make sense of it.' He took out the glass diary and flipped carefully, thoughtfully through the delicate pages.

'Still no luck understanding it?' Martha asked.

'Oh I can read it all right. Understand it, though? That's a toughie.' He brandished the diary. 'Great Hall, I think. Time to get some more puzzle pieces.'

'Is he always like this?' Lady Casaubon asked Martha.

Stellman and Lady Casaubon had work to do, preparing an official Anthium response to the appointment of Orlo as chief negotiator for Zerugma and expressing grief and shock at the death of First Secretary Chekz.

Martha followed the Doctor into the Great Hall where she found him looking from the side of the room to the enormous replica of the Mortal Mirror and back again.

'What's a mirror do?' he asked.

'It reflects light, so you see a – well, a mirror image reflected in it. Is that what you mean?'

'Good enough,' he conceded.

'So, what's the problem?' Martha went and stood beside him. She could see herself and the Doctor both reflected in the mirror at the other end of the room. 'God, I look a mess.'

'That's just your reflection. The real you is a lot tidier.'

'Thanks.'

Despite the banter, the Doctor was frowning. 'So,' he said, 'watch me in the mirror. If I put this down on here…' He took the glass diary and placed it on a small table at the side of the room. The table was covered with a faded velvet cloth that hung down. The Doctor squared up the diary carefully, then walked briskly back to where Martha was standing.

'Then, from here,' he said, 'we should be able to see it reflected in the mirror, right?'

'Right,' Martha agreed, still watching the reflection. 'And we can.'

'Ye-es. I was afraid you'd say that.'

Martha brushed a stray strand of her hair back with her fingers. Was it her imagination, or was there a slight lag? The tiniest delay before her reflection did the same?

'And if you keep looking at the book, the diary. Or rather, if you keep looking at its reflection...'

'Yes, doing that.'

'And you lower your gaze ever so slightly to look *under* the same table...'

'OK.'

'You'll see – what?'

Martha stared. The cloth hung down low, but from where she was standing the angle was such that she could see the stone floor beneath the table and the edge of the wall behind. 'I see the floor, the wall, that's it. What am I supposed to see?'

'Nothing under the table?'

She shook her head.

'So, if you now turn to look at the real table, and not the reflection in the mirror, you'll see quite clearly...'

The Doctor was watching Martha as she turned, as she looked under the table. As she heard the sound of a child's barely suppressed laugh.

As Martha saw – quite clearly – that under the table was a small fair-haired girl.

Martha turned back to the mirror – nothing. 'But, that's impossible.'

The Doctor was smiling and nodding. 'Isn't it, though?'

Martha turned back, and saw Janna crawl out from under the table. She whipped round to check the mirror – the empty mirror. The mirror that did not show the small girl who was laughing and running from the room.

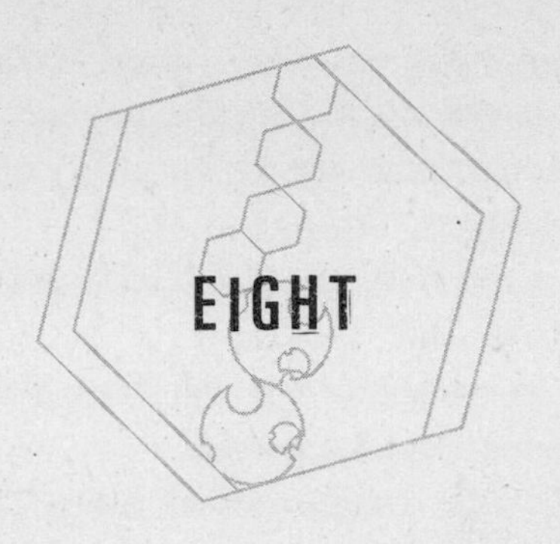

EIGHT

'That is seriously weird,' Martha said. The Doctor had already set off across the room, and she had to run to catch him up.

'Only sort of weird that counts,' the Doctor said.

'Where are we going?' Martha asked.

'To find Janna.'

'And ask her why she doesn't show up in the mirror?'

'Always assuming she knows,' the Doctor agreed. 'There are probably a fair few things we ought to be asking her. Don't you think?'

Martha didn't answer. She was breathless just keeping up with him as they sprinted down the corridor.

'Oh,' the Doctor said when he got no answer. 'You don't.'

He skidded to a halt at a junction. The corridor emerged into an open area with a high, vaulted ceiling.

Several doors and three other passages led off from it.

'Which way did she go?' Martha gasped.

You try down there,' the Doctor said, pointing along one of the passages. 'I'll take this one.'

Martha pointed to the third passageway. 'What's wrong with that one?'

'All right, you take that one and I'll try along there.'

'But what if—' Martha started.

'OK, OK.' The Doctor patted his pockets. 'Coin, coin…' he muttered.

'We're going to toss a coin to decide? That doesn't seem very scientific.'

The Doctor abandoned his search for a coin. 'True,' he agreed. 'You want scientific?'

Martha nodded. 'Please.'

'Right.' He pointed at each of the three possible passages in turn, intoning: 'Dip red white blue, who's it – not you. OK, so not that one. I'll take this one, you go down there.'

He set off rapidly down the passage before stopping so abruptly he nearly fell over, and turning back to Martha. 'Sorry – you happy with that?'

Martha smiled. 'Of course.'

'See you back at the Great Hall,' the Doctor yelled over his shoulder as he disappeared.

Martha set off more sedately along her passageway. She didn't hold out a lot of hope of finding Janna, and she suspected that as much as anything the Doctor just wanted to be active – to be doing something. That was probably what kept his brain working. If they didn't find the girl, he'd come up with another plan…

The man with the shattered hand stepped out from the shadowy depths of an alcove at the back of the Great Hall.

He had heard the Doctor and Martha, had seen them chase off after the girl Janna. They were getting too curious, he thought. Discovering too much. But the Doctor had made a mistake. He had left the glass diary on the side table where the girl had been hiding. He would have to be fast, as they could be back at any moment. In and out as quickly and quietly as possible. No time even to wake the sleeping shock troops. But they would hear the Doctor when he came – when he fell into the trap, and into their hands. Their *claws*…

The man hurried across the room, listening for any sound of the Doctor and Martha returning. But there was nothing. He picked up the glass book and turned to the mirror. The mirror in which he cast no reflection.

He walked more briskly now. Stood in front of the mirror. Reached behind the frame and adjusted a control. Then he stepped into the mirror. The surface rippled like dense, silvery liquid as he passed through, into the world beyond. Taking the diary with him…

General Orlo insisted on being there when the GA commander, Colonel Blench, reported to Defron. Not that there was anything much to report.

'We are continuing to search the castle for any intruders,' Blench told them. 'All the guides are being questioned as well as the rest of the staff. Obviously we will need permission to search the delegates' rooms.'

'You think we are suspects?' Orlo demanded.

'Not at all. As I understand it, sir, all the delegates were in the negotiating chamber awaiting the First Secretary when the incident occurred.'

Orlo's scaly skin curled back from his teeth. 'Incident? Is that all it is to you, Colonel?'

'I can assure you my troops and I are treating this with the utmost diligence and seriousness,' Blench said calmly. 'I can call it a murder or a killing or an assassination if you wish, but in my experience emotive terminology makes for an emotive response.'

'No one is questioning your dedication or efficiency,' Defron said quickly.

'Though I assume there are as yet no positive results to report from this diligence and efficiency?' Orlo said.

'The General is experienced enough himself to know that negative results are also important,' Blench said levelly. '*Not* finding incriminating evidence or a possible weapon in the places we have so far searched narrows down the options.'

Orlo met the colonel's stare for several moments before he replied. 'You are right, of course, Colonel Blench. I have the utmost confidence in your ability and your dedication. Forgive my impatience, but First Secretary Chekz was a friend as well as a colleague. I served under him for a time in the Wensleyan Campaign.'

'I didn't know that,' Defron said.

'I'm not sure Chekz knew that,' Orlo said. 'It was a long time ago, and I was new to the Zerugian Marine Force. Thank you, Colonel. You may go.'

Colonel Blench saluted and left. If it occurred either to him or to Defron that it was not Orlo's place to dismiss an officer of the Galactic Alliance, neither of them said so.

There was an echo to Martha's footsteps. She didn't want to frighten Janna away, but what if it was the mysterious monk? Martha paused, half-turned, and heard a stifled giggle.

It was Janna.

Martha turned quickly, but the passageway seemed empty.

'I know you're there,' she called. 'I heard you, Janna. I just want to talk. The Doctor – remember the Doctor? He wants to ask you some things. About the mirror.'

'What about it?' Janna's voice came from the other side of the corridor from where Martha had been looking.

'I thought...' Martha shook her head and turned to face the girl as she stepped out from behind a pillar.

'That's my sister. She's following me, and I'm following you. But she's dead, so ignore her. Ignore her and maybe she'll go away.' The girl turned and shouted at the empty shadows across the corridor. 'I wish you'd go away!'

'It's all right,' Martha told her. She hurried to the girl

and hugged her close, felt her tiny fragile body shaking with emotion and fear. 'It's OK. You're quite safe. I'll look after you. I promise. Don't be scared by... the shadows. You'll be all right.'

Janna pulled away after a moment. Her lips were pressed together tight in a determined expression. She nodded quickly. 'Course I'll be all right. I'm always all right. What do you want to know, then?'

Martha reached out. The girl hesitated, then let Martha take her by the hand. 'Come with me, back to the Great Hall. Is that OK?'

Janna nodded quickly again. Then she glanced into the shadows opposite before pulling her hand free and running on ahead of Martha. 'Come on then. Race you!'

The path the Doctor had taken led him back to the living accommodation. He walked past his own room and Martha's, already pretty sure that he had lost Janna. With any luck, Martha would find the girl.

Before long he found himself walking down a twisting stone staircase that led past Gonfer's room. On an impulse, he knocked at the door. There was no answer.

'No one here but us monks,' he murmured, and continued on his way.

Only to meet someone coming up the stairs towards him. A shadow fell across the curving wall, distorted and grotesque – claw-like hands reaching out. The Doctor stopped.

'Who goes there?' he asked brightly.

A figure dressed as a monk appeared round the corner. It stopped as it saw the Doctor. Slowly, the figure reached up and pushed back the heavy hood of its cloak. To reveal the grinning face of Gonfer.

'Hi Doctor,' he said. Then his smile froze and he looked round nervously.

'Oops,' the Doctor said. 'Hood off, but still in costume.'

'You won't tell?' Gonfer whispered nervously.

'Not in a million years. And you know when most people say that they don't mean it. But I do. Every second of every minute of every hour…'

'Thanks,' Gonfer hissed before the Doctor could move on to the days and months and years and beyond.

'Have you got a few minutes?' the Doctor asked, backing up the stairs to let Gonfer up to the landing and into his room. 'Only I'd like your help with something.'

'Sure. What do you want?' Gonfer asked as he shrugged off his monk's habit. 'They made me pay for the one I lost,' he said glumly. 'Docked my wages.'

'That's a bit harsh,' the Doctor agreed. 'Wasn't your fault. You tell them. Or I will, if you like.'

'We're not supposed to leave our quarters,' Gonfer said. 'But I had a shift due in the courtyard so I went to check if we're allowed out yet. Apparently not. But, I guess it'll be all right if I'm with you. So, how can I help?'

'By reflecting, really.'

'You want me to think back to when I was attacked?'

'No, no, no.' The Doctor grinned. 'Not that kind of reflecting. I want to know if I can see you in the mirror in the Great Hall.'

It was completely bizarre.

Martha could see herself in the mirror, but Janna standing right next to her just wasn't there in the reflection. Martha put her arm round the girl's shoulder – and in the mirror, her reflection put her arm round… nothing. Was it Martha's imagination, or did her own reflection have a knowing smile that she herself lacked? Come to that, how would she tell?

'Do you see yourself in the mirror?' Martha asked.

Janna shook her head. 'It's just empty. I can see you though. With your arm out. You look silly.'

'Yeah,' Martha agreed, and withdrew her arm. 'What about other mirrors? Do you appear in them?'

The girl shrugged and skipped off round the long table, apparently bored with the whole thing.

Martha turned back to the Mortal Mirror, trying to outstare herself – like that was going to happen. Over her reflected shoulder she saw the Doctor and Gonfer come into the room.

The Doctor stopped and sighed. 'Well so much for my big theory.'

Martha turned. 'What theory is that?'

'I wondered if it was an effect of the environment.'

'You mean Janna's reflection is gone because of something here in the castle?'

'Maybe a side effect of the force bubble and the way it allows light through, I thought,' the Doctor said. 'Well, that was the theory. Could have been some sort of light-wave sickness, maybe. I don't know. But since Gonfer here shows up loud and clear...' The Doctor was standing by Martha now. He leaned forward and peered into the mirror. 'Is my hair really like that?'

'Pretty much.'

He nodded thoughtfully, before deciding: 'Good. Good, it looks good. Don't you think it looks good?' he asked Gonfer over his shoulder. He didn't wait for a reply but turned back to the mirror, licking his palm and slicking down his quiff. 'Still looks good.'

'Get over yourself,' Martha said, laughing.

'Right.' The Doctor clapped his hands together. 'Better get thinking about Theory Number Two then.' He turned to wave at Gonfer and smile at Janna. Then his smile froze.

'What is Theory Number Two?' Gonfer asked.

'The diary. The glass diary. I left it on the table when we followed Janna.' He patted his pockets frantically. 'Sure I did. Did you see me? I didn't pick it up again. Did you pick it up again?'

Martha shook her head. 'It was there. I didn't touch it.'

Gonfer went and looked under the table. Janna stopping skipping and running round the room to watch him, her head tilted to one side with interest.

Martha tried to remember what the Doctor had done.

The diary was not there now, but she remembered him putting it down. That must have been when he saw that Janna was under the table. So just before he asked Martha to look at the table in the mirror and tell him what she saw.

She turned back to the mirror, and looked again at the reflection of the table. The velvet cloth hanging over the edge, the patch of floor dimly visible beneath.

The glass diary resting on the velvet cloth.

Martha snapped round, checking the table. No diary. Yet – in the mirror…

'Doctor,' she said. 'Look – in the mirror. It's in the mirror.' She reached out to point to the reflection of the diary that wasn't there. She was close to the mirror, close enough to touch it. Her fingers brushed against the surface.

And went through it. Ripples of liquid reflection at her fingertips.

'Martha!' the Doctor yelled from behind her. She could see his reflection – distorted by the ripples – as he ran towards her. 'Martha, don't!'

But she couldn't stop herself. It was so strange, so compelling. She leaned forward, over the frame and into the mirror. She felt the cool surface of the looking glass close round her, heard a tearing sound as reality split open, and she stepped into the room beyond.

The silvery surface closed round Martha, and she was gone. The Doctor saw his reflected self running towards him. Neither slowed down. Both met with a metallic clang, and he bounced back off the mirror and stumbled away.

'Martha!'

He ran back to the mirror, hammering on the cold, unyielding surface.

'Martha – I'll get you out of there. Don't move, don't do anything, I'll get you out!'

The room was like a dimly lit version of the Great Hall. There was no sign of a reflected Gonfer or Doctor. Martha was alone.

Holding her breath with a mixture of awe and fear and trepidation and excitement, she walked slowly forward. Would that work? It seemed to. Alice, when she went through the looking glass in the story, had to walk *away* from where she wanted to go, but Martha found herself walking across the Great Hall just as if she was really there.

Except everything was reversed. She raised her hand, half thinking it would be her other hand which moved. But that worked too.

'Doctor!' she exclaimed. 'It's weird. Come and see.' She turned back, expecting to see him following. Or perhaps standing the other side of the mirror behind her, like it was a window.

Except that there wasn't a mirror behind her. There was just an empty alcove, at the back of which was a solid stone wall.

Martha ran back – thumped at the wall. Felt the dusty stone flaking under her fists as she yelled and shouted for the Doctor. The Doctor who wasn't there.

She was trapped in the world behind the mirror and there was no way back.

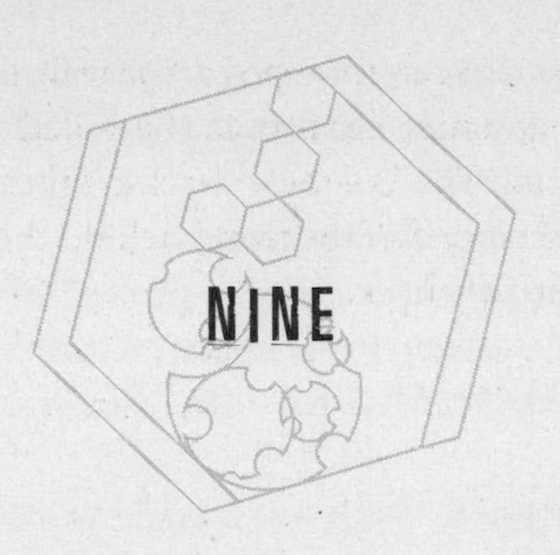

NINE

The Doctor checked over every inch of the mirror, and then started on the frame.

'It's just a mirror,' he said. 'An ordinary mirror. Or rather, it isn't. Obviously. As it swallows people up.'

'How can it do that?' Gonfer asked. 'I mean, there's just a wall behind. Where did she go?'

'Some sort of portal. Maybe remote activated, set to allow one person, and only one person, through before switching off again.' The Doctor stepped back and tapped his chin thoughtfully. His reflection did the same. 'The diary's gone,' he noted. 'So it is just a mirror again now. But I still can't see Janna.'

He swung round to check she was actually there. The girl was sitting cross-legged on the stone floor watching him with interest.

'What does that mean?' Gonfer asked.

'It means there are degrees, levels of mirror-ness to it. It's behaving *almost* like a real mirror. Almost, but not quite. Why is that?'

Gonfer shrugged. 'Don't ask me.'

'Sustaining another image, a projection? Something from inside the mirror that's been extruded into the real world just like Martha's been absorbed into the looking glass?'

Janna frowned. 'There was a man,' she said.

'A man?'

'He came out of the mirror.'

The Doctor crouched down beside her. 'Did he? You saw him?'

'I was hiding, under the table. This man came in and looked at the mirror and his reflection...' She looked away.

'Yes?' The Doctor was beckoning with his fingers, encouraging her to tell him more. 'Yes, yes, yes?'

'His reflection had a gun. And shot him.'

The Doctor's fingers stopped moving. 'Oh. And then the man came out of the mirror.'

Janna nodded.

'Then what?'

'I watched him push the body back into the mirror. I waited till the man had gone. I went to see the body, but it wasn't there. It wasn't in the mirror. Then I ran away to my den and I hid.'

The Doctor sucked air through his teeth. 'Yeah, well, that's probably what I would have done.' He straightened up. 'Who was the man?'

'Don't know. One of the important people. I still see him. He's still here.'

'Or his reflection is.'

'His reflection?' Gonfer said.

'Well, not strictly his reflection. But a mirror image. that is, an image from the mirror. Could be someone else entirely, could be anyone – or anything. It just looks like him. Like a mirror image of him. But it could be someone else, clothed in the light of his reflection. A disguise for whoever he is. The mirror can become a portal – a doorway into... somewhere.'

'Where?' Janna asked.

'A pocket universe, a finite space, another world. Must be a *tiny* world – you'd need huge amounts of energy to sustain anything big. I wonder where it gets the energy from, it isn't connected to anything.'

He ran back to the mirror and examined the frame. He pulled it carefully forward from the wall and peered behind. 'Found the controls,' he announced. 'Encoded access. And a deadlock seal on the security pad.' He stepped back and threw his arms open. 'It must use light. I bet it uses light. That'd be brilliant, using light.'

'For what?' Gonfer asked.

'Energy. Light *is* energy. Convert the protons that hit the mirror's surface. Maybe capture their kinetic energy. Or potential energy... No,' he decided, 'that would make the mirror turn black. Heat maybe?' he shook his head in a sudden violent movement and waved his hand as if to clear the air. 'Doesn't matter. We can worry about that later. First we need to get Martha back.' He leaned towards the mirror and shouted: 'Can you hear me, Martha? Be with you in a tick. Soon have you out of there. Promise. Cross my hearts.'

'We could get Bill and Bott to smash it open,' Janna said.

'I don't think that's a very good idea.' The Doctor caught sight of Janna's disappointed look. 'But thanks for the thought.' He had his sonic screwdriver in his hand. 'I've got a better idea though. Something a bit less drastic. If a man can come out of the mirror, then so can Martha.'

'You can get her back?' Janna said, jumping to her feet in delight.

The Doctor's grin was enormous. 'Oh yes.'

There was something very different about the place, though it took Martha a while to work out what it was. Then it struck her, so suddenly that she said it out loud.

'There's no smell.'

She sniffed, drawing in a deep breath of empty air. The whole place smelled empty – of nothing at all. It was like drinking distilled water – you thought water from the tap had little taste until you tried pure water. Then you realised that what you thought was 'nothing' was a whole mixture of different subtle flavours. Distilled, pure air – was that it?

Or is it just that smells don't have reflections, she

wondered. Was that what she was now – just a reflection, somehow split from her actual self? Was another version of Martha, *real* Martha, still out in the Great Hall with the Doctor? The thought made her feel dizzy and faint. Was this for ever?

'No chance,' she muttered. There had to be some other way out, a way back. Martha looked round. The flickering lights cast only a faint glow, the whole room was in semi-darkness. The doors at the end of the Great Hall were standing open and she could see into the passageway outside.

'So what's beyond the reflection?' she wondered, walking slowly towards the open doors.

'It's all to do with refraction,' the Doctor was saying as he tied the sonic screwdriver in position. He'd had to use a lace from one of his shoes, looped through the frame of the mirror and holding the sonic screwdriver angled towards the surface. 'Agitate the mirror at just the right angle, and that will stimulate the systems and...' He stepped back to admire his work. 'And there you go. Well, there I go. You'd better stay here.'

'Why can't we see Martha in the mirror?' Janna asked.

'You can talk!' the Doctor said, looking from the girl to the empty space where her reflection wasn't. 'But we will. Once I...' He reached for the sonic screwdriver. Then, abruptly, he pulled his hand away as if frightened he might get burned.

'What is it?' Gonfer asked.

'We can't look,' the Doctor said. 'If it's a refractual technique, then the protons are giving off potential energy – energy from light they haven't yet reflected, you follow?'

'No,' Gonfer and Janna both said.

'No,' the Doctor agreed. 'Not sure *I* do either. But if we *see* Martha in the mirror, actually inside it – then she'll never get out. It'll fix the refraction. Just observing her changes the world she's in, and imprisons her inside. That's what happened to Manfred Grieg,' he realised. 'Even if you did get out, you'd be…' He wiggled his lower jaw as he considered. 'Actually, I don't know what you'd be. But it wouldn't be good, that's for sure. One way or another you'd be trapped.'

'I still don't understand how she got in there,' Gonfer said. 'If she is in there.'

'I don't know where else she'd be. Someone set the mirror, primed it to allow one person through then it shut down again.' His eyes widened. 'And they put the diary in there. Someone came and took it and put it in the mirror world knowing we'd see it. *I'd* see it. Oh Martha,' he realised, 'it *was* a trap. A trap for me. I am so, so sorry.'

'But we'll get her back,' Janna said.

'We will. And then I've got a few questions for General Orlo.'

'Orlo?' Gonfer said.

'Starting with,' the Doctor said, 'did he know when

he offered it that this is the actual real Mortal Mirror and not a copy? Or is he being duped like the rest of us?' He adjusted the sonic screwdriver and turned to face Gonfer and Janna. 'Right, you two get out of here. Shut the doors and don't let anyone in. No one must see what happens in the mirror or we'll both be trapped inside, right?'

'Right,' Gonfer said. 'But what about you – won't you see Martha before you step through?'

'I'll close my eyes,' the Doctor decided. 'That's desperately dangerous for a man with only one shoelace, but sacrifices have to be made. I'm hoping only sentient recognition will trap us inside. I mean, some dust mite or spider or even a mouse or something is bound to see us in the mirror. But so long as they don't know what they're looking at we should be OK.'

'What if you're not?' Gonfer asked.

'Well, if we're not out and calling for you in half an hour then you might want to think about getting some tea. Then do as Janna said, and get Bill and Bott to smash the mirror.'

'But you said that would trap you inside,' Janna told him.

The Doctor nodded. 'And not just us, I suspect. If we're not back, it might be best if nothing came out of the mirror ever again.'

Beyond the patch of corridor visible through the doors, there was nothing. Or so it seemed. As Martha peered into the darkness, though, she realised there was something – vague shapes in the gloom.

She felt her way carefully along, glancing back to the doors and what light there was, afraid that at any moment she might be swallowed up by the shadows and cease to exist. With every tentative step she took she could hear the sound of her own breathing echoing rhythmically in her ears.

She was in a corridor – just like the corridor outside the real Great Hall in the real castle Extremis. Only shrouded in darkness. She felt her way along, hand on cold stone wall, feet scuffing on the flagstone floor. Her breathing seemed to be getting louder.

Her hand felt the change from stone to wood, the give as the door she was pressing on swung slowly open. Martha stepped carefully, tentatively into the dark room. The air seemed to breathe round her – sighing and blowing like a breeze.

Shapes loomed either side like pews in the nave of a darkened church. She gingerly reached for the nearest of the shapes. It was angular and hard to the touch. Wood. The end of a bed.

Martha froze. Realisation crept over her, cold and unpleasant – it wasn't only her own breathing she could hear. She could hear breathing coming from the bed. From all the beds. She was in some sort of dormitory.

Her eyes were adjusting now and she could make out the space between two of the beds – a low cabinet. Something hanging from a rail… An armoured tunic that glinted as it caught a sudden flare of light.

Not a dormitory. A barracks.

Scaly reptilian skin caught the flickering light.

A great yellow-eyed head rose from the nearest bed. Sharp teeth flashed as the great jutting jaw moved.

'Is that you, Sastrak?' a voice growled. 'Is it time?'

Martha backed slowly away, retracing her steps. The light behind her blinked out. The Zerugian's eyes continued to glow in the dark, turning, searching Martha out.

Then a hand came down on her shoulder, twisted her round. Another clamped across her mouth before she could cry out.

The Doctor pulled her gently back into the corridor, and Martha let out a sigh of relief as soon as he removed his hand.

'Sorry,' he whispered. 'Don't think we want to wake them up. Must be pretty boring for them hiding out here. In the dark. Can't even play cards, poor things.'

'That light – sonic screwdriver?'

He shook his head. 'That's keeping the mirror open so we can get out again. It was a match.'

'It burned for a long time.'

'Everlasting match,' he said, as if there could be no other sort. 'There's not a lot of light here. Which is sort of how it works, of course. The mirror takes light energy from the protons on the way through.'

There was faint, flickering light coming from down the corridor, from the open doors to the Great Hall. The

Doctor's dark, silhouetted shape licked his finger and held it up as if testing for a breeze.

'And we're actually *inside* the mirror?'

'We're actually inside the mirror. You want time to reflect on that?'

'As much as you need time to think up some new jokes.' But she was grinning back at him in the dim light. 'Weird how there's no smell, isn't it?'

He let her go into the Great Hall first. 'Is this a new joke coming?'

'Let's just get out of here,' Martha said.

Across the Great Hall, Martha could see there was now a mirror hanging in the alcove – exactly where there had not been one earlier. In it, or through it, she could see the Great Hall, the real Great Hall.

The Doctor took her hand. 'Come on. Just remember, as we go through, keep your eyes closed. We mustn't look at each other.'

'Right. Why not?'

'If either of us sees the other one in the mirror, they'll be trapped here for ever. Or what comes back through the mirror won't be the real thing. I'd rather not find out which theory is correct.'

'Oh great.'

'You go first,' the Doctor hissed. 'And whatever you do, don't look back. Even this side, once we're in the light from the mirror, once we're close to the threshold, it might make a difference. Just walk forward, and whatever you do, whatever happens, don't look back.'

Martha started slowly towards the mirror, straining to hear the Doctor's footsteps behind her. 'Why not hold hands?'

'Not sure if it can cope with the mass of two people at once.' He sounded further away. Wasn't he following her? 'Another theory I'd rather not put to the test.'

'Right,' she muttered. 'You still there?'

'Right behind you. I've just got something to do. Won't be a minute.'

'What?' She almost turned round, but forced herself not to look.

'Don't look!'

'Doctor – what are you doing?'

No reply.

'Doctor?!'

Still nothing. Or was that the sound of footsteps? Of claws scraping on stone? Heavy Zerugian breathing? The first sharp touch of a cold claw on the back of her neck?

'Don't turn round – don't turn round,' Martha said to herself, over and over. Out loud, but not too loud: 'Doctor!'

Still nothing. Just a strange, shuffling sound – a foot dragging on the floor. Like some misshapen ghoul lumbering after Martha. Anything – it could be anything behind her...

Martha reached the mirror. She looked out into the Great Hall beyond. Saw how the image rippled and distorted as she reached into and through it. Heard the tearing of the fabric of space as she stepped out into the Great Hall. The *real* Great Hall.

'Can I turn round yet?'

Silence.

'Doctor – can I turn round?'

Then a rippling tearing sound as *something* came through the mirror behind her.

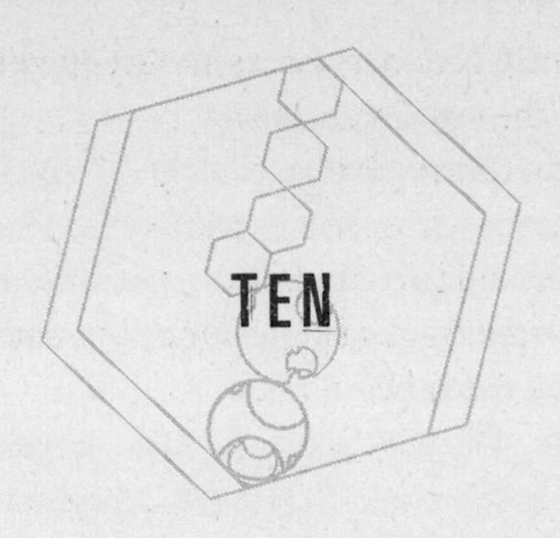

TEN

The *something* landed just behind Martha. 'It's only me,' it said. 'Nearly lost my shoe there. That'll teach me to take the lace out. Still, I remembered to pick this up.' The Doctor was holding the glass book, the diary Martha had gone into the mirror for in the first place.

Martha almost sobbed with relief. 'Thank God for that. Thank God it's *you*. I thought...' She hugged him tight for a moment.

'What's that for?'

'For being you.'

In the mirror, the Doctor and Martha watched the embrace. Standing separate. Reflections that did not mirror the action in the room.

'Ah,' the Doctor said seriously, disentangling himself. 'Should have thought of that.'

He reached up quickly for the sonic screwdriver,

attached to the frame of the mirror by his shoelace. The reflected Doctor reached up too.

But not for the sonic screwdriver. A hand rippled out of the surface of the mirror, grabbing the Doctor's wrist. The reflected Doctor's face was contorted in rage. His voice was a vicious snarl – the Doctor's, and yet not the Doctor's: 'Let me out!'

'No,' the Doctor gasped. His fingers clutched desperately at the sonic. Scrabbled, caught it. Wrenched it away from the mirror.

Martha caught the Doctor as he stumbled back. He was still aiming the sonic at the mirror, the tip of the device glowing blue. The surface of the mirror shimmered and the protruding hand of the mirror-Doctor disappeared with a tearing scrape of sound.

The images in the mirror stared out at the Doctor and Martha. The mirror Doctor was still enraged. The reflection of Martha hurled herself at the mirror. The real Martha flinched as her reflected self crashed into the surface, like hitting a glass window. She staggered back.

'They're trying to get out,' Martha said.

'Mmm,' the Doctor agreed. 'I've closed the gateway between the worlds. Just need to sort out the osmosis damper.'

The Doctor in the mirror was hammering furiously, soundlessly, on the other side of the looking glass.

'Can they break the glass?'

'Hope not,' the Doctor said. But he didn't sound very sure.

Martha in the mirror crouched down, trying to push through – her palms hard against the glass. Her mouth was moving – pleading silently with her real self.

'Let me out... Let me out!'

She looked frightened more than anything.

'Why are they trying to get out?' Martha said. 'They're just reflections, aren't they?'

'They don't know that,' the Doctor said. 'Dark reflections. Distillations of aspects of our character – anger and fear, by the look of it. The mirror focuses what we felt when we were inside, like a lens. It's as true a reflection as a distorting mirror at a funfair. That said...' He sounded almost sad as he watched the figures in the glass. '... If you were trapped in there, wouldn't you want to get out?'

Martha knew the answer without having to think about it. A life inside the dim, odourless, restrictive world she had so recently experienced?

The Doctor aimed the sonic at the mirror. 'I'm sorry,' he said quietly. 'I'm so sorry.'

And, abruptly, the image in the mirror changed. The pitiful sights of Martha trying to push through the mirror, of the Doctor hammering on the glass, were gone. The Doctor was aiming the sonic. Martha was standing, mouth open, a tear welling up in the corner of one eye.

'It's just a mirror,' the Doctor said quietly. 'Let's hope it stays that way.'

***

Gonfer was visibly relieved when Martha followed the Doctor from the Great Hall. She thought for a second he was going to hug her, but he shuffled awkwardly and restrained himself. So she hugged him instead.

'Thanks for your help.'

'It was nothing. No problem, really,' he said, embarrassed.

The Doctor was looking round the corridor, peering into alcoves and turned to stare at shadows. 'Where's Janna?'

'I think she got bored,' Gonfer said.

'I told you both to stay here.'

'That's all right. I told her I could manage.'

'No, no, no – that's not the point. I wanted to talk to her. I hadn't finished. There's stuff I need to ask her. Like, tons and tons of stuff.'

'What about?' Martha asked.

'She saw a man come out of the mirror. Well, that's not good. Not a man, probably either.'

'A Zerugian?'

'Maybe. But something that used the reflected light to make an image for itself. If she saw it in the mirror and it still came out...' The Doctor turned back to Gonfer. 'Definitely need to talk to Janna. So, where did she go?'

He shook his head. 'I don't know. She has hidey holes and dens all over the place. Or the gardens.'

'Try her den,' the Doctor said to Martha. 'Then the gardens. But keep to the paths, yes?'

'Yes,' Martha agreed. She looked at Gonfer.

'The paths are safe,' he assured her. 'I'll come with you.'

'You'll stay here, like I asked,' the Doctor told him. 'Keeping watch. I haven't finished in there yet.' He turned back towards the Great Hall. 'There's a lot I haven't finished. Haven't finished talking to Janna, haven't finished sorting out that mirror. And before I can do that I have to finish reading the diary.'

'And why is the diary important?' Martha asked.

'It's Manfred Grieg's account of how he was trapped in the mirror.'

'So? We know that, don't we?'

'Do we? If he was trapped in the mirror, why didn't we meet him? Why wasn't he there with the red carpet and brass band keen to welcome us and make our stay long and enjoyable?'

'Who says he wasn't? Maybe we just didn't see him.'

'And how,' the Doctor went on without pausing, 'did his diary find its way out of the mirror and so conveniently behind a stone in the castle?'

'Maybe it was never in the mirror,' Gonfer said.

'Yes,' Martha agreed. 'Maybe it's just a story, or a fake.'

'It's not a fake,' the Doctor said quietly.

'How do you know?'

'Because you can only read it when it's reflected in the mirror.'

'Even so…'

'And because it's made of glass.'

***

There was no sign of Janna in her hidden den, or anywhere nearby. Martha stood in the passage outside the secret door and listened. She knew the girl liked to hide and watch what was going on, and she seemed to have enjoyed following them. But there was no sign of her now.

Martha thought she glimpsed one of the guides, face hidden beneath his monk's hood, but when she looked again there was no one there.

She made her way back out into the castle courtyard. Beneath the starry sky, she found Bill and Bott replacing one of the stone steps on the stairs leading up to the battlements.

'We only did this one a couple of hundred years ago or so,' Bill complained.

'Tell me about it,' Bott said.

'OK. It was about ten in the morning, and we'd just...'

'I don't mean *tell me about it* tell me about it,' Bott said. 'I mean, like, tell me about it.'

'Sorry to interrupt,' Martha said before Bill could respond. 'But have you seen Janna?'

'Frequently,' Bill said.

'Often,' Bott agreed.

'I actually mean recently.'

'You're looking for her?' Bill asked.

'Obviously.'

'We'll help,' Bott offered. 'Got to be better than replacing steps that we only did a couple of hundred years ago anyway and shouldn't need it for another couple of hundred.'

'Tell me about it,' Bill said.

'No – don't start that again. I'll be fine,' Martha told them. 'The Doctor wants a word with her, that's all. So, if you know where she is...?'

'Do we know where she is, Bill?' Bott asked.

'We might do, Bott,' Bill said.

'Good.'

'And there again we might not,' Bill went on.

'Oh, do me a favour,' Martha sighed in frustration.

'What sort of favour?' Bott asked. 'Normally we don't do favours.'

'Normally it's work,' Bill said. 'Not favours. Favours implies choice.'

'No one gives us a choice.'

'I'll give you a choice,' Martha said. 'All right? The choice is do me a favour and tell me where Janna is – if you know.'

'Or?' Bill asked.

'Got to be an "or",' Bott said. 'Not a choice without an "or" is it?'

'Or don't.'

Bill looked at Bott, and Bott looked at Bill. Each nodded at the other.

'She's in the garden,' Bill said.

'Looked like she was heading for the maze.'

'Thank you.' Martha hurried towards the main gates out into the castle grounds.

Then she had a thought, and turned back to the robots. 'Is the maze mined?'

'I didn't mine it,' Bill said. 'You, Bott?'

'Not me, Bill. Who mined the maze?' Bott asked Martha.

'Well, I don't know. Maybe no one. I just want to know – is it safe?'

'Always has been,' Bill said. 'No mines in the maze, if you didn't put them there.'

'But keep to the path on the way,' Bott told her. 'It should be OK, but the mines were cleared by GA Sappers.'

'What are they?'

'They're robots,' Bill said, a hint of disdain in his electronic voice.

The same disdain was in Bott's tone as well. 'Never trust robots,' he said.

> *The woman Martha followed the little girl into the garden. She wasn't sure where she had gone.*

From the main gate, Martha could look down over the grounds and gardens spread out before her. They sloped gently away to the abrupt horizon where the small world ended. Formal lawns, rose garden, and the hedges that she knew from seeing it from above formed the maze.

> *She shielded her eyes from the harsh light as she sought out the girl, Janna.*

There was no point in running off into the gardens – even if there were no lurking landmines to avoid. She'd do better to watch for any sign of Janna. Shielding her eyes from the light of the bright floodlights high above, Martha looked out across the beautiful landscape, searching for any sign of movement.

She didn't have to wait long. There – among the trees that lined the far side of the lawn. Something moved. Was it Janna? It was worth a look. Provided she kept to the path she would be all right.

Martha kept telling herself that she would be all right. She didn't know if the mines were buried or if you'd be able to see the tips of the detonators poking through the ground. But she kept a careful eye on where she was putting her next step every inch of the way.

Somewhere ahead of her, someone laughed. A high-pitched tinkle of sound, evaporating into the air as Martha looked round for its source.

As she did so, she caught sight of the girl – a flash of fair hair catching the light. At the edge of the maze – just for a moment. Then gone, vanished behind one of the tall hedges. How had she got over there so fast? And without Martha seeing her.

> She saw her by the trees, and then entering the maze. Or rather, she thought she did.

The laughter came again. And again, it seemed to emanate from the trees ahead of her. A trick of the acoustics, she decided. Maybe the planet – or asteroid or whatever the lump of rock floating in space was called – maybe it was so small that Janna's laughter had travelled right round it and so seemed to be coming from the opposite direction.

'Walk away from it to get there,' Martha murmured, reminded again of Alice and her adventures in the looking glass. She set off carefully towards the maze.

There was a wide, gravel pathway that led from the trees and the rose garden beyond across to the maze. Martha kept to the path, right to the middle of the path, scouring the ground in front of her, and feeling more nervous with every step. She'd be happy once she was in the maze. The maze would be fine. Gonfer had said it would be fine. And Janna was in there.

What could possibly happen to her in a garden maze?

The Doctor turned the thin, brittle pages slowly and carefully as he read. And with every page he became increasingly worried.

'This diary is old,' he told his reflected self – who fortunately agreed in every corresponding movement. 'It was walled up for a hundred years or more. It feels old. Yet…' He turned another page. 'Yet this is an entry for *today*. How can that be? Could he foretell what was the future when he wrote it?'

The words on the page were clear in the mirror as the Doctor read. As the Doctor felt the beats of his hearts quicken.

The woman Martha followed the little girl into the garden. She wasn't sure where she had gone. She shielded her eyes from the harsh light as she sought out the girl, Janna. She saw her by the trees, and then entering the maze. Or rather, she thought she did.

The maze. It was just as originally planned in the drawings that Krunberg had made all those years ago. Planted by the Henderson brothers, it had grown so high that Martha could not see over the hedges. Which was always the intention, of course.

Inside the maze, Martha stopped, uncertain which way to go. She turned, and was startled to see

The Doctor held his breath as he turned the glass page, and held it up to see its reflection in the mirror.

As soon as she entered the maze, the hedges seemed to close in around Martha. The quality of the light was somehow different. Dappled green shadows played across the ground ahead of her. She now had no idea which way to go.

There was some theory about always turning left, wasn't there? Or was it that you kept your left hand always in contact with the hedge?

Martha reached out, and found the hedge was surprisingly soft. So – start by going left.

As she turned, a figure stepped into the maze beside

her. The cloaked and hooded figure of a monk. He turned slowly towards Martha, the space under his hood a dark emptiness. His cloak dappled green like the ground.

'Who are you?' Martha said, her voice quieter and more nervous than she'd intended. She took a step back as the monk approached.

When the monk spoke, his voice was also quiet. It was ragged and sharp and rasping, as if he was talking through broken glass. But it wasn't the monk's voice that made Martha's blood run cold and her throat go dry. It was what he said to her:

'Greetings, Time Traveller.'

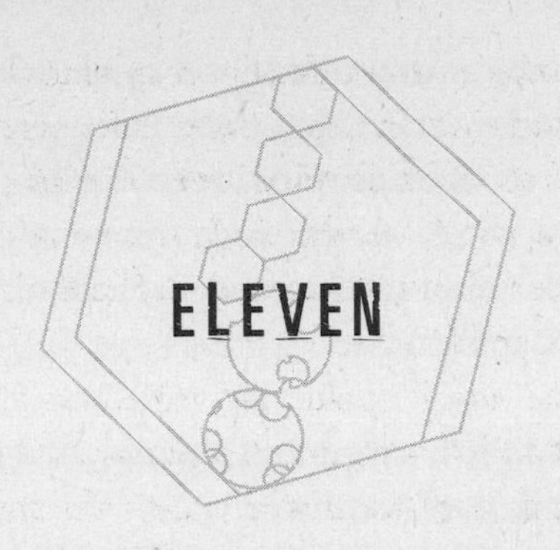

ELEVEN

Martha backed away from the cloaked figure. Something gleamed in the darkness under the hood as the figure stepped towards Martha.

She turned and ran.

'Left, always go left,' she told herself as she ran.

She had no idea who the monk was, or what he wanted. But he'd been stalking her and the Doctor, and he'd bashed Gonfer on the head. She wasn't sure quite what she had seen glinting under the hood, but she wasn't about to wait around and find out.

She had to find Janna – maybe the girl would know what was going on.

But where was she?

Martha pulled up, gasping for breath. She'd not heard the monk following her, not seen him behind her. She struggled to control her breathing, and listened.

The tinkling sound of laughter came from the other side of a hedge. The foliage was dense and leafy, but Martha forced her hands into it and pulled aside small branches to try to see through. She could make out the shape of Janna on the other side. Her fair hair was shining gold in the light from the huge lamps in the sky above.

'Janna!' Martha called through the hedge. 'Janna, I need to talk to you. Stay there.'

But the girl was already running off, and Martha was unable to hold the hedge apart for any longer. The branches were straining to regain their shape. The leaves closed over the view of the little girl skipping off along the green corridor.

The hedge was too high to climb, and too thick to push through. So Martha had to follow the maze. She caught a glimpse of Janna peeping back at her from round a corner. But by the time she got there the girl had gone.

Almost immediately, Martha heard a laugh from behind her. She spun round – and there was Janna again. This time at the other end of the hedge. Again, a glimpse, then she was gone, leaving only the faint echo of her laugh. How had she done that? How could she get from one end of the hedge to the other so fast? Martha ran to look, but there was no path on the other side between the two points.

Unless she could somehow get *through* the maze. Remembering the hidden door in the wall of the castle,

Martha pushed at the hedge. But it was just a hedge, and all she gained from the effort was a series of scratches across her hands.

Never mind. She'd ask Janna what she'd done – and how she'd done it – when she caught up. It seemed to be a game to the girl. A cross between Hide and Seek and Follow the Leader.

'Dip red white blue,' Martha murmured. Then she set off deeper into the maze.

> The further into the maze Martha went, the more lost she became. Her only hope was to find the little girl, who might be able to show her the way out again. But she was aware too of the strange hooded figure who had tried to speak to her.
>
> And it seemed to Martha that it was not only one little girl she was following. It seemed to Martha that perhaps – just perhaps – the girl's dead sister was there in the maze with them. A ghostly figure behind the hedges, laughing and playing and keeping to the shadows. Close to where she had died...

The Doctor shut the diary. That was the last entry. And if what was written somehow reflected what was actually happening out in the gardens, then that was a worry.

Walking briskly, the Doctor pushed the diary into his pocket. It was a worry on so many levels, he thought. How could an old diary – and it was certainly old, he could *feel* it was old – how could it describe events that were happening right now? How could it mirror – and he chose the word deliberately – reality?

Without making a conscious decision, the Doctor broke into a run. He needed to find Martha. He needed to get to the maze.

Another thing that was odd about the book, he thought as he pelted through the castle corridors, his rapid footsteps echoing off the stone walls, was that the style changed. There was a distinct difference between what was written by Grieg when he was trapped in the mirror, and what was written about the current events inside the castle. They became less personal, related in the third person, as if by an observer rather than the central character. Had they been written by someone else? Or did Grieg think his role in the unfolding of his own story had changed?

Nearly there now – nearly at the door out into the castle courtyard.

The Doctor rounded a corner, and almost slammed into Defron coming the other way.

'Excuse me!' the Doctor announced loudly as he executed an impressive sidestep. 'Coming through!'

'Doctor – wait,' Defron said, grabbing his sleeve.

The Doctor pulled up. 'Is it urgent?'

'Well, yes.'

'Then I can give you ten seconds. No more. Martha's in trouble.'

Defron nodded as he took this in. 'Ten seconds, er –

right. The Galactic Associated Press Corps ship is about to arrive. General Orlo and Lady Casaubon have agreed to hold a press conference in the Great Hall. Announce good progress on the treaty, show how willing both sides are to make this work.'

'Feel the hand of history on their shoulders?' the Doctor suggested. 'Good stuff. And what about the small matter of a murderous assassin being on the loose?'

'The official line is that Chekz died suddenly and tragically of natural causes. Colonel Blench will keep everything locked down and secure.'

'Fine. Great.' The Doctor was bouncing on the balls of his feet. 'That it?'

'I'd like you to be there,' Defron said. 'In case of any, you know, awkward questions.'

'Incognito.'

'Absolutely. Visiting expert or something.'

The Doctor frowned. 'Ye-es...' There was something stirring at the back of his mind, but there was no time right now to tease it out and see what it was. 'Keep us good seats,' he called over his shoulder as he ran on. 'Near the ice cream queue.'

Although Martha struggled to understand how it was possible, she realised that the explanation was simple.

She also realised that despite her intention of keeping to the left, the glimpses of Janna and the tantalising echoes of her laugh had led Martha to stray from that intention. There was no way she could confidently retrace her path to the entrance of the maze, so she might as well keep going after Janna and hope to catch her up.

After all, if this was just a game, maybe Janna would tire of it and come and find Martha.

The path she was on led to a dead end. Martha could see the blank green wall of the hedge in front of her. Just as she was about to turn and try another way, she saw that there was an opening just ahead of her. Hedges behind hedges – it meant that you had to be close to the openings before you even saw they were there.

She stepped through and found herself in a large square. The centre of the maze. The middle was paved with a chequer board of stone slabs, alternately polished white and deep red. The focal point was a weathered statue on a large square plinth. The carved shape of a massive Zerugian warrior looked down disdainfully. The reptilian creature was clothed in battle armour and brandishing a fearsome-looking gun. Its teeth were chipped and worn, and the base of the statue was crumbling with age.

As she approached, Martha saw a shadow emerging from behind the statue. Not the shadow of the statue itself, it was the wrong shape, it was in the wrong place. And it was moving – slowly disappearing out of sight as someone hid behind the massive stone base.

'Got you!' Martha declared, and sprinted round the statue.

She expected to find Janna hiding there, laughing,

hand pressed to her face in a mixture of amusement and embarrassment at being caught.

Instead, the cloaked figure of the monk stepped forward, blocking Martha's line of escape to the gap in the hedge.

'Oh,' Martha said. 'It's you again. What do you want?' she demanded, defiant.

In reply, the monk unfolded his arms from the sleeves of the cloak. He held something up – something that glinted and shone as it caught the light.

Martha gasped in astonishment. But the sound was lost in the blast of the explosion.

The Doctor sprinted down the causeway leading from the castle's main gates into the grounds.

'Maze, maze, maze,' he said to himself, shielding his eyes and scanning the landscape until he saw it.

If he stuck to the path, he would have to head off towards the rose garden, then double back. Much further than the direct route across the lawn and past the edge of the lake.

He didn't hesitate. Sonic screwdriver in hand, he set off at a jog. The tip of the screwdriver glowed blue as he angled it at the ground ahead of him. It bleeped rhythmically.

Suddenly, the rhythm changed. It became more insistent, higher in pitch, as it detected a hidden mine. The Doctor changed course slightly, and the rhythm returned to the steady pace it had originally had.

Halfway there. Another change of rhythm, and another change of course.

Over halfway.

Then an insistent, sudden, rapid beeping. Changing course seemed to make no difference, and the Doctor stopped abruptly. He swept the screwdriver in an arc in front of him. There was no way through.

With a sigh, the Doctor adjusted a setting, and aimed the sonic screwdriver.

The air was split with the deafening roar of the explosion as the mine detonated.

The ground shook with the force of the blast from somewhere outside the maze. Martha staggered, and almost fell.

The monk clutched at the base of the statue for support, almost dropping the glass book he was holding. The diary.

'How did you get that?' Martha demanded as the sound of the explosion died away. 'What have you done to the Doctor?'

'You ask me how *I* got it?' the monk countered in his rasping voice.

There was another explosion.

The monk was knocked backwards as the ground shook. He clutched the book tight, and struggled to keep his balance. But the movement shook his hood back from his face.

His gleaming, broken face.

Martha stared in horrified disbelief at the old man. His thinning white hair was like ice, moulded to his head. His face was lined and worn – every facet of it catching and reflecting the light from above. A thin crack ran from his forehead down to his chin, and there was a chip out of his nose, another gouged from his chin. A hole scooped from his cheek.

Just a glimpse. A nightmare moment before the monk pulled his hood forward again.

'Have you read the diary?' the monk asked. He stepped towards Martha. 'Have you been into the mirror?'

'Who are you?' Martha said. Her throat was dry and it was an effort to swallow. 'What do you want? Keep away from me!'

The monk hesitated. The head turned in a quizzical manner. He seemed to be about to speak again.

Then Janna ran from the entranceway, from behind the monk, and hurled herself at him. The girl's shoulder cannoned into the back of the cloaked figure, sending him sprawling. His foot caught and twisted, and he fell.

Martha grabbed Janna. The monk had fallen between them and the way out, so she dragged the girl behind the statue, gesturing at her urgently to keep quiet. The monk's hood had fallen forward over his face, so he had not seen Martha and Janna hide.

Peeping out cautiously from behind the plinth, Martha saw the monk haul himself to his feet. He had one hand pressed to his face as he staggered away, out of the central area and back into the maze.

'Why did you run away from me?' Martha hissed to Janna.

The girl's eyes were wide in surprise. 'I didn't.'

'Why didn't you stop, or come when I called to you?'

Janna shook her head in surprise. 'I followed you,' she said. 'I saw you go into the maze. That monk man too. I thought you might need help, so I followed.'

'But you came in here first,' Martha insisted.

Janna looked back at her, impassive. 'You are so strange,' she said. Then she skipped out from behind the statue and across to the paving where the monk had fallen. 'What's this?'

Martha could see it too – something on the ground, where he had fallen. Something that caught the light and shimmered and gleamed and shone.

Janna picked it up. She held it out to Martha.

'It's glass.'

'Must be from the book.' Martha took it carefully from the girl. But it was the wrong shape. Too thick and curled to be from the pages or cover or even the spine of the diary. 'He must have dropped it,' she murmured. She held it up to the light, seeing the tiny cracks deep inside the old glass.

'What do you think?' she asked as a shadow fell across the ground at her feet.

But Janna had gone. The shadow was the Doctor's. He took the glass from her and examined it. 'I think this place is amazing,' he said. 'An amazing maze. Best sort. And I think we should get back to the castle before the press corps arrives in force. And I think,' he said, tossing the piece of glass into the air and catching it again, 'that our troubles may be just beginning. What do you think, Martha?'

'I think,' she told him, 'that Janna's sister is still alive.'

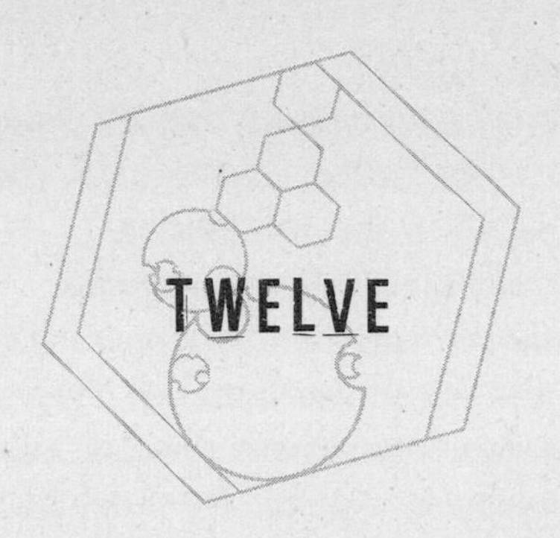

TWELVE

The Doctor paused at an intersection of several hedges. 'Yes,' he decided at last. 'This way.'

'I followed her into the maze, you see,' Martha explained. 'Only Janna said she followed me. And it certainly seemed like there were two of them.'

'Identical?'

'Twins.'

'No,' the Doctor said. 'No, that's not right at all.'

'I'm just telling you what I saw.'

'Oh not you,' the Doctor assured her. 'No, I think it must be back this way.' He spun on his heel and set off in the opposite direction.

'Isn't there some scheme where you keep going left or something?' Martha asked.

'That'd work,' the Doctor agreed. 'Except we just went right. And it does rather assume the hedges stay put.'

'The hedges move?!'

'Well, I don't know. Be fun if they did though. I was in a maze once...' the Doctor started to say. Then his voice faded as he paused at the next junction.

'Dip red white blue?' Martha suggested.

'Or eeny meeny miny mo.' He tapped his finger on his chin. 'I wonder which we should do. Perhaps we need to do one-potato two-potato to work out if it's best to go eeny meeny or dip red.' He shook his head. 'Two routes, two choices, two little girls. And,' he added, 'two murders.'

'Two?'

'Chekz, and the man Janna saw looking in the mirror – whoever he was.'

'Defron, maybe?' Martha said, following him along his chosen path – straight to a dead end, and then back again.

'Or one of the soldiers. Or Stellman, or... Who do you think? Colonel Mustard in the Great Hall with the Mortal Mirror? Colonel Blench – there's a thought. He's the commander of the GA troops. Nice man, for a soldier. What do you reckon, Martha?'

'Well, I'm no expert...' Martha started.

'No,' the Doctor agreed. He sounded thoughtful.

'Oh, cheers for that.'

'Oh, but yes.' The Doctor turned quickly and punched her lightly on the shoulder. 'Yes you are, Martha. You're brilliant. You're trained and everything. You can tell if someone's dead.'

'Yeah, well that's not usually the desirable option. By then it's too late.'

'Never too late. Never say die. Well, hardly ever. Well, not much anyway. Though in this case…'

'Doctor – what are you on about?'

'The thing is,' the Doctor said, 'does it matter if Tylda really died?'

'It matters to Janna.'

The Doctor nodded. 'Maybe that's the point. She's going out of her mind being haunted by the ghost of someone who isn't dead.'

'You think someone's doing it deliberately?'

The Doctor shrugged. 'Why bother? Seems rather convoluted as plans go. If you want to discredit her, you just need to say she's wrong.'

'About what?'

'About what she saw in the mirror? Who knows. And anyway, why would Tylda hide from her own sister?' He clapped his hands together. 'Right here we are – just through here.'

Martha followed the Doctor through a gap in the hedge. But her growing relief turned to disappointment as she saw the open square area with the large statue of a Zerugian warrior on a plinth in the centre.

'Or not,' she said.

'That's good,' the Doctor said, nodding thoughtfully.

'Good? We're back where we started.'

'I know where I am now.' He pointed. 'This way. Come on.'

He led her unerringly and without hesitation back through the maze and, in what seemed like only a couple of minutes, they were back at the main entrance.

'I wonder who I need to see to apologise for the mess,' the Doctor said.

Martha could see what he meant. Two areas to the side of the lawn had been churned up, mud and soil strewn across. 'Landmines?'

'Nasty things,' he agreed with a sniff.

'You think Tylda survived the explosion, all that time ago?'

'I don't know,' the Doctor admitted. 'I wonder if it matters? Well, it matters to Janna obviously. And to Tylda. And if it does matter, does *that* matter?'

'OK. Seriously confused now.'

'So we need to get an expert opinion.'

'And that's me, right?'

'Before the press people arrive,' the Doctor went on.

His words were all but drowned out by the massive roar of the huge spaceship that forced its way ponderously through the shimmering bubble of the sky above and came in to land on the other side of the castle.

As soon as the Doctor and Martha reached the courtyard, Defron hurried over to them.

'I am so glad I found you.'

'Nice to see you too,' the Doctor said. 'Are we late for tea or something? I'm sorry. Crumpets?'

'What?' Defron looked from the Doctor to Martha

and then back to the Doctor again.

'Are there crumpets for tea? With jam? Got to have jam.' He turned to Martha. 'Haven't you?'

'Oh yeah.'

'Essential. Don't tell me there's no jam.'

'Doctor,' Defron said seriously, 'I do appreciate the value of maintaining a cover, really I do.'

'A cover?'

'Pretending to be eccentric and, well, a bit daffy.'

'Doctor Daffy Duck,' Martha murmured.

'While of course underneath the pretence you are a coiled spring of razor-sharp intelligence observing every minute detail and planning every nuance of strategy.'

The Doctor sighed. He brushed mud from his lapel. 'You've rumbled me.'

'So, tell me please – what should I say to the press?'

Martha was astonished. 'You want the Doctor to tell you what to say to the press? I thought you were the expert at that.'

'But about the assassination. What information do I – can I – release?'

'For the moment, tell them nothing. Well, almost nothing. That is, very little.' The Doctor held his thumb and forefinger close together to show exactly how much Defron could say. 'Nasty accident, regrettable incident, all under control, that sort of thing.'

'And that the GA team is actively investigating?'

'If you're pushed, you can say that, yes. Good luck.' The Doctor clapped him on the shoulder.

'But, you won't be there? Observing?'

'Got to maintain our daffy cover,' Martha said.

'You taking the Mickey, Mouse?' The Doctor looked very pleased with himself.

'Very good,' sighed Martha.

'And where will you be?' Defron asked.

'Investigating.' The Doctor took Martha's arm and led her back towards the doorway into the castle.

'But you will be there for the ceremony?' Defron called after them.

The Doctor swung through 180 degrees, pivoting Martha round him as he headed back to Defron. 'Of course. Absolument. What ceremony?'

'After the press conference. In a couple of hours. The ceremony in the Great Hall to officially open the negotiations and sign the preliminary treaty documents.'

'Live on telly?' the Doctor asked.

'Galactic News will be covering it, yes.'

'Millions watching? Just the place for a great gesture from one side or the other?'

Defron shrugged. 'I suppose so.'

'You don't think…' Martha said slowly.

The Doctor put his finger to her lips. 'We'll be there,' he said. 'And we want ice cream tubs in the interval. Chocolate, strawberry, raspberry ripple. The works.'

'I'll talk to Hombard in the kitchens.'

'One other thing,' the Doctor said.

'Yes?'

'A girl died. A girl called Tylda. A while ago. She was killed by a landmine out in the grounds.'

'Is this important?'

'She's dead,' Martha said sternly.

'Well, yes, regrettable, condolences. But does it impinge on the current situation?'

'Might do,' the Doctor said. 'So, how do I find out more about what happened?'

'Talk to Colonel Blench. As the GA Force commanding officer, he has access to all Castle Extremis security archives. He's in the Security Centre making final arrangements for the ceremony.'

Colonel Blench's thin moustache twitched slightly, but otherwise he showed no surprise at the Doctor's request.

'We'll see what records we can find,' he said before giving instructions to a soldier sitting at a large computer console. 'I warn you, there may not be much. Despite being on the front line, in recent times internal security here has been woefully lax.'

'Searching now, sir,' the soldier said as he worked at the keyboard. 'Looks like there are some still images of the event. Nothing much. Three-line report, which says just what you've told us, Doctor.'

'Defron has filled me in a little on your role,' the Colonel said. His eyes flicked across to include Martha in his comment. 'Are you anticipating any trouble at the ceremony?'

'Should we be?' Martha asked.

'After the death of Secretary Chekz? You tell me.'

'So long as you're ready for anything,' the Doctor said.

'Accessing those pictures now,' the soldier called.

'We're ready,' Blench confirmed to the Doctor. 'Give us the release codes and we'll do the job. Whatever it is.'

'Excellent,' the Doctor said. 'Er, release codes?'

Blench was leaning over the screen as the images appeared – three overlapping pictures. So he didn't see the Doctor and Martha exchange puzzled looks.

'For release of weapons,' Blench said. 'As you know, we're on a safety footing. So we'd need a formal release of weapons from you political guys.'

'Ah, of course,' the Doctor said. 'Never trust soldiers with guns. Wise policy. So you need official sanction for use of force from an accredited GA representative.'

Blench laughed. 'I don't know about accredited. But if you have the code that unlocks my soldiers' weapons, then that'll do just fine.'

'Because without it,' Martha said, wanting to be sure she'd understood this properly, 'the guns won't work.'

'That's right. So it's a good thing we've got you here in case things do go wrong.'

Martha forced a smile. 'Isn't it just.'

'There's certainly something wrong here,' the Doctor said. He was examining the three pictures, which the soldier had arranged next to each other on the screen.

'What is it?' Blench asked.

'Martha?' the Doctor prompted.

Martha examined the pictures. They showed the twisted, broken body of a girl – a girl exactly like Janna. They were unpleasant and unsettling anyway, but even more so as it seemed she was looking at the girl she knew.

'Well, she's certainly dead,' she said. Sadly, it didn't need much medical training to know that for sure. 'There's no way that girl is still alive.' She turned away.

'I was looking at the mud, here.'

'The ground's pretty churned up,' Blench said. 'Effects of the blast. It's a pretty standard disruption pattern by the look of it.'

'And here?'

'The area was shielded by the poor girl's body. So the ground is still intact.'

Martha forced herself to look. There was still grass growing where the Doctor was pointing. And footprints pressed into the grass, exposing the mud beneath.

'Looks like she was on tip-toe,' Martha said.

'Colonel?'

'Looks like she was running.'

'Even though she knew the area well, she also knew it was dangerous. Why was she running? Why wasn't she picking every step with care?'

'Maybe she *was* tip-toeing,' Martha said.

The Doctor tapped the screen thoughtfully. 'Can you pull back? Is there more of the background on the image?'

The soldier at the keyboard nodded. 'Can do. It's just grass and mud though. I thought you'd want—'

'Just do it,' Blench said.

'Sir.'

The view of the image zoomed out. The girl's body was tiny and alone on the broken ground.

'Now zoom in here.' The Doctor pointed to an area close to the body, between the girl and the wall of the castle just visible from the high angle of the camera.

The image zoomed in again. They all leaned forward, peering at the footprints stamped into the ground.

'There's two sets of prints,' Martha realised.

'She was running,' the Doctor said. 'And someone was chasing her.'

'There's no images or video of the actual event,' the soldier said. 'So we'll never know if that's true. Or who it was. Or why.'

'Unless Gonfer knows,' Martha said.

'With respect, Doctor,' Colonel Blench said, 'this happened a long time ago. Before the treaty negotiations were even considered. Are you sure this isn't just a distraction?'

'A distraction?' Martha said angrily, pointing at the screen. 'Look at the pictures. Look at what happened to her.'

The Doctor put his hand on her arm. 'The Colonel may be right,' he said quietly. 'We need to know what happened, not least so we can help Janna put it behind her and move on. But maybe we *are* getting distracted.

The press are here, there's this ceremony in an hour or two. There are more urgent things.'

'Like what's happening in the mirror?'

'Like shutting down the mirror.'

'What mirror?' Blench demanded. 'What are you talking about?'

'Nothing for you to worry about,' the Doctor told him. 'I hope. Just an attempt to sabotage the talks and stage a coup live on telly.' He held up his sonic screwdriver. 'Nothing a couple of undercover GA Agents can't sort out in a jiffy.'

'You think the Zerugians inside the mirror are a sort of fifth column?' Martha asked. 'Ready to come out and fight behind enemy lines, sort of thing?'

The Doctor led the way through Castle Extremis. They were heading for the Great Hall, by way of Gonfer's quarters.

'Perfect place to hide an army.'

'But why in a mirror?'

'Where better? Activate the portal between the mirror world and our own and out they come. No one will guess, and the scanners – even if they were up to the job – don't scan glass.'

'General Orlo?'

'I don't know. Not for sure. OK, he provided the mirror so it seems likely. But why kill Chekz? He seemed as upset and surprised by that as anyone.'

'Someone else then?'

They had arrived at Gonfer's rooms, and the Doctor didn't reply. He knocked on the door, and moments later Gonfer appeared.

'Oh,' he said. 'Hi. I'm supposed to be getting ready for this ceremony. We're all being roped in to act as guides and hand out refreshments and stuff. Nice to be allowed out of our rooms again, really.'

'Tell us what happened to Tylda,' the Doctor said quietly.

Gonfer shrugged. 'There was an accident. I told you before.'

'No, you didn't,' Martha said. 'You said she ran into the garden. You didn't say she was being chased.'

Gonfer looked pale. 'I told you, she upset one of the kitchen boys.'

'You said she ran off,' the Doctor said. 'You said no one dared to follow her into the grounds. But someone did, didn't they?'

Gonfer nodded. 'That last day. The kitchen boy – she was always playing him up. Always teasing, bullying. I think he'd just had enough. We all had, really.'

'So he chased her,' Martha said. 'And he didn't stop when she ran into the gardens.'

'He was so angry,' Gonfer said. 'He was close behind her. He thought, I suppose, that he could see where she was putting her feet and he just kept following.'

Martha could see Gonfer's eyes moving as he spoke. As if he was watching the girl running, the kitchen boy close on her heels.

'I guess she panicked when she realised he was going to catch her. Who knows what he'd have done to her if he did.'

'But he didn't catch her, did he?' Martha said quietly. It wasn't hard to guess how the story ended. And she'd seen the pictures.

'No, he didn't.' Gonfer turned away, unable to look at them as he spoke. 'She strayed from the safe path across the lawn. The explosion knocked the boy off his feet and blew out the windows in the East Wing.'

Martha reached out and put her hand on Gonfer's shoulder. 'You saw it happen, didn't you?' she realised. The pictures were bad enough, but Gonfer had known the girl, had known the kitchen boy too, wherever he was now.

'I saw it happen,' he echoed. 'Now I do what I can to help Janna. But she'll never get over it. Not ever.'

They left him alone with his memories.

'So we just turn off the mirror thing and that's it?' Martha asked.

'Well, the controls are deadlock sealed so I'll have to work out how to shut it down gracefully.' The Doctor grinned. 'But yes, that's about it.'

'And that traps the Zerugians inside.'

'For the moment. We can always let them out later.'

'And we'd do that – why exactly?'

'Would you want to spend longer in there than you have to?'

'But they're planning to kill everyone at the conference. Aren't they?'

'They're soldiers. I think they're just obeying orders. Which is no excuse, but since Colonel Blench's soldiers are in effect unarmed I don't think there'd be much of a fight. Not here at any rate. But once they have control of Castle Extremis, Anthium is only a metaphorical stone's throw away. Nothing else in the way to prevent them just rolling in.'

'Invasion?'

'Conquest. But we'll stop them.'

The Great Hall was empty, the doors standing open.

'I guess the canapés and drinks are somewhere else then.' Martha's voice echoed in the empty room.

They walked slowly towards the mirror – which looked exactly like an ordinary mirror. Martha found it hard to believe that she had actually been *into* the mirror, been trapped inside it.

'Right,' the Doctor announced. 'Bit of a delicate operation, but for a genius like me it shouldn't take too long. Just shut down the Mortal Mirror and we're done.'

'Go on then.'

The Doctor had his sonic screwdriver in one hand, and in the other he was holding the glass diary. He flipped it open and held it up to the mirror to see the reflected writing.

'There was a bit in here about how the thing works. I only skimmed through it, but with a bit of luck it'll give us some clues about shutting the thing down again...'

Something moved. In the reflection, behind the images of Martha and the Doctor. Martha caught just a glimpse, as the Doctor flipped over another thin, brittle, glass page. A flicker of motion. Where was it?

She peered into the mirror – and saw that something was moving on the side wall of the Great Hall.

At first she thought it was one of the suits of armour, poised on a plinth in an alcove. Then she realised it was just the figure's sword. As she watched, the sword lifted free, as if of its own accord.

'Doctor!' She pointed at the reflected sword, now catching the light as it twisted towards them.

'Mmm?' He turned to look at her. Saw over her shoulder. Froze.

Tearing her gaze from the sword dangling impossibly in the air in the mirror, Martha also turned.

The sword was held by a man – the expert and historian Thorodin. He angled it towards the Doctor and Martha.

'You can't stop us now,' he snarled.

The flickering light danced along the blade of the sword. It reflected off Thorodin's hand, off his face.

Martha checked the mirror – and saw that he cast no reflection.

When she turned back, Thorodin was charging towards them. His left arm raised behind him balancing his sword arm. And Martha saw that the trailing arm had no hand. It ended in a broken, ragged stump, facets reflecting the light like mirrors.

The sword sliced through the air. The Doctor spun away, but not quite fast enough.

The blade caught the Doctor's hand, as he parried with the only thing he had. The sword jarred on the glass book and sent it spinning across the room. The Doctor and Martha both leaped back.

With an explosion of sound, the diary hit the ground and shattered into fragments. The floor was strewn with shards of broken glass, glittering and shining.

Just as Thorodin's face was glittering and shining. The sword arced again, ready to slash down.

The Doctor sucked his fingers, looking annoyed more than scared.

And Martha stared at the man in utter disbelief – the man who cast no reflection in the mirror.

'He's made of glass,' she gasped.

THIRTEEN

'Are you the man in the mirror?' the Doctor demanded as he backed away. 'Was it you following us?'

Martha was backing off too, but away from the Doctor. If they kept separate, Thorodin would have two targets to deal with. One of them should be able to get to the door and go for help.

'I don't know what you're talking about,' Thorodin said, turning and swinging the sword as he tried to keep both of them in view. 'And, you know what? I don't care.'

He charged at the Doctor again, who stepped nimbly aside. 'I'd offer you a hand,' he said. 'Only I gave it back to Stellman. It was your hand, wasn't it?'

Thorodin didn't answer. He thrust the sword at the Doctor again, and again the Doctor dodged aside at the last moment.

'No idea what I'm on about?' the Doctor wondered. 'Got you stumped has it?'

'That's awful,' Martha told him. She leaped out of the way of the backswing as Thorodin wielded the sword once more.

The glass man missed the Doctor again. The sword smashed into one of the suits of armour. The armour collapsed in a clanging heap. The helmet bounced across the floor. A sword clattered, and the Doctor snatched it up.

'Ha-ha!' he cried. 'Have at you.' He raised the sword, but it was a heavy and cumbersome gesture. 'Ah, no – hang on.' The metal gauntlet from the armour was still attached to the handle, and the Doctor tugged it free and tossed it away. He tested the weight of the sword as he waited for Thorodin to close in. 'That's better. Have at you!' he tried again.

They were blocking the route between Martha and the door as they fought. She tried to edge round and past a couple of times. But, on each occasion, Thorodin swung at her, and Martha was forced to retreat.

The Doctor seemed to be enjoying himself. He easily parried Thorodin's sword thrusts, but was unable to get through the man's guard. They circled each other warily and attacked again.

Thorodin lunged suddenly forward. The Doctor was up against the long table and was forced to lean back over it. Blades locked, and the Doctor managed to force Thorodin back. But not for long. Thorodin thrust again, and the Doctor leaped backwards – up and onto the table.

'Got you now!' the Doctor declared. He swung the sword down at Thorodin.

The glass man stepped back, and the sword continued down, biting deep into the side of the table at the Doctor's feet. He heaved at it, but the sword was stuck.

And Thorodin was coming at him again.

'Time for Plan B, Martha,' the Doctor shouted.

'What's Plan B?'

The Doctor was tap-dancing out of the way on the table as Thorodin's sword swept at him. 'It's what you do when your first plan goes a bit wonky.' He leaped back off the table. 'And this is looking pretty wonky to me.'

'No, I mean – what's Plan B? What is it? What do we do?'

The Doctor backed away as Thorodin came at him again. He was standing close to Martha now. 'I was kind of hoping you'd been working on that while I was busy.'

Thorodin hurled himself at them, shrieking in rage, sword raised.

'Run!' Martha yelled.

'Yeah,' the Doctor agreed, racing after her, Thorodin at his heels. 'That'll do it. Good plan.'

Martha reached the doors from the Great Hall ahead of the Doctor, and turned to see how close he was. How close Thorodin was, too.

As she turned, she saw a blur of movement between the two men. Thorodin was bringing his sword down fast. It looked as though the blade would slice into the Doctor's back or shoulder.

But then what looked like a bundle of scruffy rags rolled out from under a side table and tangled in Thorodin's feet.

The man went flying. His sword skidded across the floor. The bundle unrolled and resolved itself into the shape of a young girl, who leaped to her feet and dashed after Martha and the Doctor.

'Janna!'

Thorodin crashed to the floor. His scream cut through the air like broken glass. Martha watched, horrified, unable to look away. The Doctor running towards her, Janna close behind. And Thorodin, pushing himself up from the floor. Looking at her. His face cracked across from the top left of his forehead to under his chin on the right, one half slightly misaligned with the other. He staggered to his feet, and scooped up his sword. He held it awkwardly in crazed fingers.

'Come on, Martha,' the Doctor yelled, grabbing her as he rushed past. His other arm gathered Janna and dragged her along as well.

Out into the corridor, Thorodin hurling himself after them, sword slicing the air. The Doctor, Martha and Janna raced along the corridor. Martha could feel the breeze on the back of her neck as the sword swept past.

Then a figure stepped out of the shadows ahead of them. Stellman.

'Doctor, duck!' he shouted.

'That's me,' the Doctor confirmed. 'Bit busy right now though. Maybe if you made an appointment?'

'No,' Martha yelled in his ear. 'He means *duck*!' She hurled herself to the floor, dragging the Doctor and Janna with her.

Stellman raised the glass gun and fired.

The gunshot was a massive echoing percussion of sound in the stone corridor. Martha looked up from the floor in time to see Thorodin's whole side smash and break away.

Another shot. The glass head exploded into fragments, and the body crashed forwards. It shattered on the hard stone floor. Shards of glass whipped past Martha's face.

Stellman walked calmly past them. He nudged one of the larger fragments of what had been Thorodin with the toe of his boot. 'Well,' he said. 'There's something you don't see every day.'

'Glass man shattered with a glass bullet from a glass gun,' the Doctor said, picking himself up and dusting himself down. 'Seems appropriate.'

'Very,' Stellman agreed. 'Considering I found it in his room.'

'You search everyone's rooms?' Martha said.

'Of course. You can't be too careful.'

'You've searched my room?' she was scandalised.

'Yours and the Doctor's, as soon as I knew you were here.'

'Can't have taken you long,' the Doctor said. 'We travel light. Good job you found that gun though,' he went on. 'Thorodin was dangerous enough with his sword. If he could have shot us, he would have. You should be grateful, Martha.'

'Oh yeah, cheers. Thanks.' She knew her room was empty, but even so she resented Stellman's intrusion.

Stellman seemed more bothered by the gun. He turned it over in his hand. 'You know, I assumed it was glass so he could get it past the weapons detectors. Now I'm not so sure.'

'It's the gun he used to shoot the real man,' Janna said. 'When he came out of the mirror.'

'You saw him?' Martha realised. 'Thorodin was the man you saw come out of the mirror?'

The girl nodded.

'He came out of a *mirror*?' Stellman said. He gave a short laugh. 'You are kidding me, right?'

'Wrong,' the Doctor told him. 'Look – he was made of glass. Of course he came out of a mirror. Where else would he have come from?'

'Stained glass window, maybe?' Martha offered.

'Yes, all right, well, I suppose that's possible,' the Doctor conceded.

'The city of glass on the glass planet of the glass people?' Stellman suggested. 'And aren't there glass deserts and a pyramid on San Kaloon?'

'Yeah, all right, so several possibilities then. But *actually*, he came out of the Mortal Mirror. And Janna saw him, didn't you?' He turned round. 'Didn't you? Janna?'

But the girl had gone.

'She doesn't hang around,' Martha said.

'She's an odd one and no mistake,' Stellman agreed. 'You know, she had a twin sister...'

'It has been mentioned,' Martha assured him.

'I think we need to find Janna,' the Doctor said. 'See what else she knows.'

'All of us?' Martha asked, rolling her eyes towards Stellman.

'What? Oh... Stellman, can you try and delay this official opening ceremony thing? Or at least get it shifted to somewhere other than the Great Hall?'

'I can try. Is it important?' He caught the Doctor's glare. 'It's important. OK, I'll do what I can.'

'And we'll go and ask Janna how come she doesn't have a reflection,' Martha said as Stellman left them. 'I mean, that's got to be important, right? Thorodin had no reflection and neither does Janna.'

'Oh, they both have reflections,' the Doctor told her. 'Or did.' He kicked aside some of the shattered glass strewn across the floor.

'Janna doesn't have a reflection,' Martha said. 'You know that. You pointed that out to me.'

'I was wrong,' he said simply. 'Janna has a reflection and you've seen it. Maybe even spoken to it. You followed it into the maze, remember?'

Bill balanced the dented helmet on top of the suit of armour he'd just finished putting back together. 'There we go. What do you think, Bott?'

'Very nice, Bill,' Bott said. He was making his way slowly round the Great Hall looking for a sword which one of the other suits of armour seemed to have mislaid. 'No sign of that sword in here.'

'Never mind. No one will notice.'

'I expect it will turn up. Things usually do.'

'You been invited to this signing ceremony press conference event, Bott?' Bill asked.

'Not me, Bill. Have you?'

'No,' Bill said. 'But I think we should be there.'

'So do I,' Bott agreed. 'We might be needed.'

'Got to keep everything nice and tidy,' Bill said. He spun slowly round inspecting the Great Hall. They had moved the long table to the side of the room and put out rows of chairs.

'Didn't like sweeping up that glass,' Bott said.

'Doesn't do my vacuum attachment any good at all,' Bill agreed. 'Nasty sharp stuff. Shan't be sorry if I never have to clear up any more glass again ever.'

'Something gets broken, Bill, and guess who has to clear it up,' Bott told him. 'Anyway, we've still got the 7.1 Quadraphonic Tarantula Surround Sound System to set up.'

'Let's get it now.'

There was an edge of satisfaction in Bill's voice as they emerged into the corridor. 'Yes, the whole castle is looking very tidy, Bott.'

'All ready for the ceremony, Bill.'

'We've done them – and ourselves – proud.'

They rounded a corner of the corridor. And stopped.

'Where the blooming heck did all this glass come from?' Bill exclaimed.

'No idea,' Bott said. 'But like I said, guess who has to clear it all up.'

'Did you manage to shut down the mirror?' Martha asked.

The Doctor shook his head. 'But now that Thorodin – or whoever it was that clothed himself in Thorodin's reflected light – now he's out of the way, there's no one to switch it on.'

'Unless he had an accomplice,' Martha said.

'Ever the optimist,' the Doctor said, smiling. 'We know Thorodin killed Chekz, or at least had a hand in it.' He paused for Martha to laugh, and when she made a point of not doing so went on. 'He clonked Gonfer over the head and then stalked after us in the monk's outfit.'

'Er,' Martha said.

'He followed you into the maze for some reason.'

'Ah,' Martha said.

'And finally, if further proof were needed…' The Doctor stopped and turned to face Martha, frowning. 'What are you doing that for?'

'Doing what?'

'"Er" and "Ah" and all that stuff.'

'Because the monk man wasn't Thorodin. I mean, I only got a glimpse of his face, but it wasn't him.'

'Er,' said the Doctor. 'Ah… Yes, I can see where it's coming from now.' He let out an explosive sigh. 'So who *is* the monk?' he demanded in exasperation.

'Why don't you ask him?' Martha suggested. She pointed along the corridor.

Further along, stepping out from an alcove into the flickering light, was a hooded figure wearing a long, dark cloak.

'Assuming it isn't one of Gonfer's mates,' the Doctor said. But from his tone, Martha could tell he didn't think it was.

Another figure stepped out of the alcove. At first Martha thought it was Janna. But as she followed the Doctor along the passage, towards the two figures waiting for them, she saw how the light reflected off the girl's face, her hair, her clothes. Like they were made of glass.

The monk reached up slowly with one hand and pushed back the hood of the cloak.

Martha recognised the face beneath, even though she had only glimpsed it before. The chipped nose, the hairline cracks across the features. A face made of old, brittle glass.

In his other hand, the monk was holding something. A book. The glass diary – but that was impossible, the diary had been smashed to pieces.

The Doctor stopped in front of the two glass figures. 'I know who you are, Janna,' he said. 'And I can make a good guess now at you,' he said to the monk.

'I am not Janna,' the girl said. Her voice was Janna's and yet it wasn't. It sounded lighter, more fragile.

'Her reflection then,' Martha said.

The girl shook her head, strands of delicate hair catching the light. 'Janna's dead. She's been dead for years.'

'What?' Martha gasped.

The monk took a step forward. 'Forgive me if I frightened you earlier,' he said to Martha. 'I am Manfred Grieg – the Man in the Mirror.'

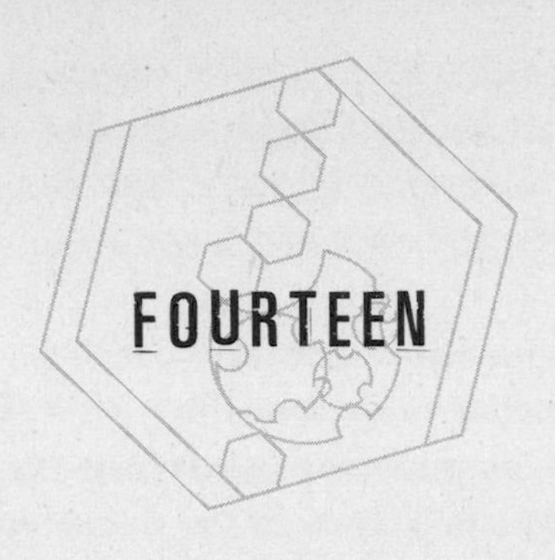

FOURTEEN

'I've read your diary,' the Doctor said. 'Quite enjoyed it. But if you want a few pointers I can help you with your prose style and grammar.'

'Maybe later,' Martha told him. 'So, who are you and what do you want?' Martha asked Grieg. 'Are you really made of glass? Glass people – I've seen it all now.'

'The mirror isn't just a portal, a doorway to another universe,' the Doctor said. 'That's the problem, isn't it? Once you're inside you're made of light – or potentially made of light. And if anyone sees you, perceives you as a light wave or a series of protons or whatever, then that rewrites your DNA as a translucent matrix based on the silicon that runs the computer chips that make the whole thing work. Probably,' he added. 'Is that it?' he asked Grieg.

The man made of old, chipped glass considered.

'Perhaps,' he said at last. 'I confess, such explanations are a little beyond me. All I know is that the mirror is not a prison. It is a trap. And that is how you must see it, Doctor – if you are to succeed. If you are to stop General Orlo.'

The girl who wasn't Janna was shifting nervously on her feet, desperate to say something. Now she blurted it out: 'Why does my sister run away from me?'

Martha crouched down so she was at eye level with the girl. 'She doesn't know who you are. She's afraid of you. She thinks you're a ghost.'

The girl laughed nervously. 'That's silly.'

'Is it any more silly than a reflection running about the place?' the Doctor asked gently. 'She'll get there. Give her time. Like Martha says, she's frightened and nervous. And since Tylda died—'

'But Tylda didn't die!' the girl said. 'She's still here, she's me and I'm her.'

'What do you mean?' Martha asked. She glanced at the Doctor, but he shook his head.

'I'm Tylda,' the girl insisted. 'It was Janna who died. It should have been me, but it was my sister. It's my fault, all my fault and now even my own self can't bear to look at me.'

Manfred Grieg put his hand on the girl's shoulder. 'Calmly, my little friend,' he said. 'Time for all that later. First, we must help the Doctor and Martha stop General Orlo.'

'You're sure he's behind all this?' Martha said. 'I mean,

Thorodin killing Chekz and everything.'

'He's the most likely suspect, Martha,' the Doctor said. 'For all his talk about diplomacy and being tired of war, it was Orlo who brought the mirror here. The real Mortal Mirror that his family saved and preserved. It's no copy.'

'Bill and Bott knew,' Grieg said.

'They said it was the same,' Martha recalled.

'They meant exactly the same,' Grieg said. 'They hung the original mirror, remember. So they knew this one was exact in every dimension, in every measurement, even its weight. The same mirror.' He held out his arms. 'I am proof, if it were needed.'

'You said that Orlo doesn't understand what the mirror is,' the Doctor said. 'I'm paraphrasing, but you said it's a trap not a prison.'

'You were imprisoned inside it though,' Martha said. 'In the story.'

'Oh, the story is true. As far as it goes.'

'I like stories,' the girl said. 'Tell us a story.'

'We don't have time for stories,' Martha pointed out. 'We need to get to the Great Hall in case Stellman can't stop the ceremony.'

'He won't,' Grieg said. 'Orlo won't let him stop it now. You see, Orlo thinks he has won. He thinks his soldiers will emerge from the mirror and he will take and hold Castle Extremis. The galaxy will witness his triumph and none will dare oppose him again.'

'Well, maybe he's right,' Martha said.

'But Orlo thinks the mirror is a prison. He thinks he has found a way to open the door to that prison, so he can hide soldiers inside and bring them out through the door when they are needed.'

'Well, yes,' Martha said.

The Doctor put his hand on her arm. 'You're saying he's wrong?'

'The door was always open,' said Grieg. 'The mirror is not a prison but a trap. Not a trap that holds you in one place and allows no freedom of movement.'

'Then, what?'

'A trap that holds you for the rest of your life. A trap that allows no escape no matter how you come and go through the portal. A trap that, once you understand it, will destroy Orlo's dreams for ever.' Grieg's eyes gleamed as he leaned forwards. 'Do you want to understand it, Doctor?'

The Doctor returned Grieg's stare. Then he dropped to the floor, landing cross-legged, patting the stone slab beside him. 'Sit down, Martha. It's story time.'

It was called the Mortal Mirror in honour of the Mortal Monks of Moradinard, who originally built Castle Extremis. But the monks had nothing to do with the mirror. They were men of peace and valued their solitude. They built this place as a retreat from the rest of the galaxy. But they built it in the wrong place.

When the Anthium fleet ventured out beyond the Visonic Belt, they realised that the star debris and asteroids in this area formed a natural barrier. The only safe route through was past the

Monastery. Fleet Admiral Karloff devised a plan – the Extremis Strategy – to buy the monastery from the Mortal Monks and turn it into an armoured fortress that would defend Anthium from any aggressor that tried to come through. And, of course, Karloff knew too that the monastery would make an ideal forward base for any attack Anthium wished to press home.

Zerugma had just been discovered. We considered the reptilian race there to be warlike and aggressive. We feared they would make war on us – and they feared we would attack them.

And the Mortal Monks refused to sell up and move on. Some argued that the Monastery was a better defence than a fortress – peace and understanding ends wars more effectively that military might and force of arms. Sure enough, as soon as Anthium moved against the Monks, so too did Zerugma. Extremis – as it was renamed – became the first battlefield. And the Mortal Monks, so aptly named, became the first innocent casualties. But by no means the last.

By the time I was appointed Chief Minister, the war was old and we were all weary. I felt that peace had at last become an option, and pressed for Anthium to negotiate with Zerugma. But we had to do that from strength, and they held Extremis. My first task on the road to peace was to take it back, and that was what I did. An act of aggression that would, I hoped, pave the way to a lasting peace.

But the Lord High Advocate for Anthium and later the Governor of Castle Extremis was a man called Kendal Pennard. And he had very different thoughts. He welcomed the stalemate created when I took back Extremis for him. And it was in his interest to prolong the status quo. When things change, then the people expect a change of leaders too. And Pennard was so very ambitious, so hungry for power.

He couldn't believe that my dreams were purely for peace, for an end to the war and the death. Especially as it was I who had devised the strategy to recapture Extremis after the Second Occupation. He thought it must be a ploy, political manoeuvring for my own gain. He thought I was after his job, and he would defend that more fiercely than he would ever defend this castle.

He thought long and hard about how he could puncture the bubble of public opinion that was growing in my favour as my part in the government and in the recapture of Castle Extremis became known. He considered reopening hostilities, but ultimately even Pennard realised that was madness. The people, now getting used to an uneasy peace, would never tolerate that.

Which gave him an idea. What if he could prove that I – Manfred Grieg – was the one who wanted war, who really hated the Zerugians and was desperate to take the fight back to them?

But it was not enough to denounce me. For all his failings, Pennard knew he needed me if he was to maintain the peace. From my negotiations and diplomacy, the Zerugians had recognised my very real desire for peace. As a result, I was the only man the Zerugians would even begin to trust. So Pennard's challenge was to strip me of my status and popularity while keeping me as an adviser. He needed a way of forcing me to work for him, to keep the Zerugians in check, while giving up all my ambitions and aspirations – as he saw it – for power. Without my help, Zerugma might again wage war and strive to capture Castle Extremis.

A prison wouldn't work. I told you the mirror was not just a prison. I was no use to him in prison, so he devised a trap. He went to the Darksmiths of Karagula and told them what he needed. They can bend any material to their will – metal, wood, plastic, glass, and even light itself. They created the Mortal Mirror – named Mortal after the Mortal Monks, and also because that was the trap. Mortality.

You know, of course, of the great feast. You know how Pennard pretended he was about to honour me and instead forced me into the Mortal Mirror. Everyone saw me – inside, cut off, hammering on the glass and screaming to be let out.

And when the feast was over and everyone was gone, I was still there, trapped in the glass. And Pennard came and spoke to me. He took a chair, and he sat in front of the mirror and he explained what he had done, and how the mirror worked. And the trap.

He told me how I could escape from the mirror. Any time I liked, I could come out and he would protect me if I worked for him. But always, I would live in fear of my own mortality. I would remember how brittle and fragile my life would be. I would live from second to second knowing that at any moment…

Grieg stopped. He stared off into space as he remembered his past.

Martha and the Doctor were sitting opposite him. The glass girl was beside them. No one had said a word as Grieg told his story.

'But, I don't understand,' Martha said. 'If you could escape from the mirror at any time, what was the point? Was he threatening to put you back in for good, or what?'

Grieg turned his head to look at her. He held up his

hand so that the light was behind it, shining through and illuminating the cracks and chips and blemishes in the coloured glass. 'This is the point.'

'They'd all seen him in the mirror,' the Doctor said. 'Just as Janna saw her own reflection.'

'I had the last laugh,' Grieg said. 'Though there was no mirth in it. Only death. I refused to come out of the mirror. He shouted and screamed, and finally begged me to come out. But I retreated into the darkness beyond the reflection, a world that reflects our own but which grows progressively darker the further you move from the light admitted by the mirror. But despite the darkness, the loneliness, I vowed never to set foot again in the real world.'

'And once you were gone,' the Doctor said, 'Zerugma went to war with Anthium.'

He nodded. 'They saw my fate – my death as it seemed – as an indication that Anthium had turned aside from the road to peace. Without me there to mediate, the war started again. Zerugma took Extremis again, and Orlo's great grandfather took the Mortal Mirror.'

'But he didn't destroy it,' Martha said.

'No. He kept it safe, until now.'

'And why have you come out of the mirror now?' Martha asked. 'After all this time?'

'Because once again there is – finally – a chance for peace. If we stop General Orlo. If the treaty negotiations go ahead in good faith.'

'You can have peace at last,' Martha realised.

But Grieg shook his head. 'Oh no. Not me. I shall never have peace. That was Pennard's trap, the curse of the mirror. As the Doctor said – I have been seen in the mirror. And so, thanks to the light-fusing technology of the Darksmiths, I am made of glass. Brittle, delicate, fragile glass. Every moment I spend in this world, I risk cracking, chipping, breaking, *shattering*. Our lives are fragile at the best of times. But now I am more fragile than ever. Every step I take, I grind down my own foot. Every moment I am here I risk my life. That was the trap.'

He stood up, and Martha saw how carefully he planned every moment. How cautiously he moved.

'Now you know.' Grieg turned to the Doctor, who was also getting to his feet. 'Now you know what to do, how to end this madness. Get to the ceremony and stop General Orlo.' He held up his hand, clenching it into a fist so tight that Martha could hear the glass cracking like ice. Grieg's features contorted in obvious pain as he held up his clenched fist. 'Make this all worthwhile,' he said.

Hurrying back to the Great Hall, Martha knew what they had to do: 'We must stop the ceremony.'

'Oh no, no, no,' the Doctor told her. 'That's just what we mustn't do. Don't you see? Orlo doesn't understand. His plan's based on a false premise. We have to let the ceremony go ahead. We have to finish this, flush them out, expose the truth.'

'Doctor, Martha – thank goodness!' Stellman came running up to them. 'I couldn't persuade Defron to postpone the ceremony. He'd already announced it at the press conference and won't lose face by changing the schedule. It's going ahead in a few minutes in the Great Hall.'

'Brilliant!' the Doctor said. 'That's terrific. The more people there to see what happens, the better.'

'But I thought—' Stellman started, hurrying to keep up.

'That was minutes ago,' Martha told him. 'He's changed his mind a dozen times since then.'

Bill and Bott were clearing away the remains of the shattered glass that had once been Thorodin as they neared the Great Hall.

'Coming through!' the Doctor yelled.

The two robots moved quickly aside. Bill had a vacuum attachment fixed to the end of one spindly arm. The Doctor leaped over it as he passed.

'Might need you in the Great Hall soon,' he called back over his shoulder.

Then he skidded to a halt. 'Might well need you actually.' Martha and Stellman waited while the Doctor ran back to Bill and Bott and talked urgently to them. 'Is the sound system all set up?'

'Set up and tested,' Bott said proudly.

'Latest technology,' Bill added.

'With a top-end range amplifier and tonal distortion matrix built in?'

'As standard,' Bill agreed.

'State of the art,' Bott said. 'And finished in chrome and black.'

The Doctor beamed. 'That is fantastic. Definitely going to be needing you.' He lowered his voice as he explained to them what he wanted. 'Soon as you can,' he finished. 'They'll be starting in a minute.'

'Happy to help,' Bott called after the Doctor, Martha and Stellman.

'Just so long as there's no mess,' Bill said.

'Maybe there aren't really any Galactic Alliance agents,' the Doctor said as they neared the Great Hall. 'Maybe it's a bluff, or Defron got the wrong end of the stick, or they haven't arrived yet.'

'Don't knock it,' Martha said. 'So long as everyone thinks it's us.'

Stellman looked from Martha to the Doctor and back again as Martha spoke. 'So, just who are you?'

'That's a very good question,' the Doctor said. 'Let's save it for later. When I can think of a very good answer.'

'We're here to help,' Martha said.

'That's a comfort,' Stellman told her. He didn't sound convinced.

The doors to the Great Hall were standing open, and there was a GA soldier on either side of them. The soldiers snapped to attention as the Doctor, Martha and Stellman passed.

Inside, the Doctor led them to empty seats near the back of the crowded hall. It had been turned into an auditorium, with a raised area at the end, in front of the Mortal Mirror. Massive speakers were arranged along the sides of the hall, and Martha could make out the tiny microphones the dignitaries on the dais were wearing. Behind her, just inside the doors, was a large sound-mixing desk like she'd seen at the back of theatres and nightclubs. Bill and Bott had sneaked into the hall and were watching from behind the desk.

'Aren't we going to stop them, or say something?' Martha asked.

Defron was on his feet, pressing his hands down on the air to gesture for quiet. The assembled press – a mixture of humans and reptilian Zerugians, as well as various other 'people' that Martha wasn't sure counted as either – became hushed.

'I'm glad I ordered ice cream for the interval,' the Doctor said. 'Where's Stellman gone?'

'Over there.' Martha pointed to where the man was walking up the aisle in the middle between the rows of chairs to take his seat on the dais. Lady Casaubon looked relieved to see him. General Orlo's expression was unreadable, but Martha was relieved to see he cast a reflection – the back of his head visible above the back of his chair in the huge mirror.

'Right,' Defron announced, 'now that we are all here, I think we can begin. I do apologise for the slight delay, which was due to circumstances beyond my control.' His eyes sought out the Doctor as he said this. The Doctor waved. Defron did not wave back.

Along the sides of the hall, GA soldiers stood impassive. The press waited expectantly. What looked like a video camera hovered silently in front of the dignitaries on the dais.

'It is no exaggeration to say,' Defron went on, 'that today marks a turning point in the history of two great nations – Anthium and Zerugma. Today, here, now, history will be made.' He gestured to a small table at the side of the room. A velvet cloth hung down almost to the stone floor, and on it was an open book.

'That must be the treaty they're going to sign,' Martha whispered.

The Doctor yawned. 'Come on, Orlo,' he murmured.

'You want him to do something?' Martha hissed.

'I want him to think he's in control. If he realises that he's miscalculated... It's a good job Thorodin never got a chance to talk to him. I hope.'

'We are about to witness—' Defron announced. But he got no further.

'Be silent!' General Orlo roared. The tiny microphone attached to his breastplate and wireless-linked to the sound desk at the back of the hall relayed his words through huge speakers arranged along the sides of the room.

Defron turned, flustered and confused. 'I beg your pardon?'

'I said, be silent.'

The General rose to his clawed feet and stepped forward. 'You are right,' he announced, adjusting his eyepatch as he spoke. 'History will indeed be made here today. But not by you.' He grabbed Defron by the shoulders, lifted him off his feet and hurled the startled man from the dais to sprawl across the people sitting in the front row.

There was confused muttering. Cameras began to flash as the press sensed a photo opportunity.

Orlo stood at the front of the dais. Behind him Lady Casaubon made to stand up, but Stellman put his hand on her shoulder. Silently he gestured for her to leave the side of the dais.

'Today you will indeed witness history.' General Orlo stared out at the audience, waiting for silence.

Martha gasped. 'The mirror – look in the mirror.'

There were murmurings as other people also saw what was happening. Heads turned, assuming that what they could see was a reflection of events in the Great Hall. But it was not.

The mirror was angled so that the press could not see themselves reflected in it. All they could see was General Orlo, alone on the dais now that Defron, Stellman and Lady Casaubon were gone. And the line of Zerugian soldiers marching through the open doors at the back of the hall.

Their heads appeared first, like the masts of ships rising over the horizon at sea. As they approached the mirror, Martha and everyone else could see the shining breastplates, the clawed hands holding their guns, the snarling dripping teeth.

Orlo turned, so that it was his reflection that spoke out of the mirror to the confused audience.

'Today, Zerugma will conquer!' he announced.

And the reflected image of Orlo stepped out of the mirror to stand beside the real General. His soldiers marching through behind them, weapons raised.

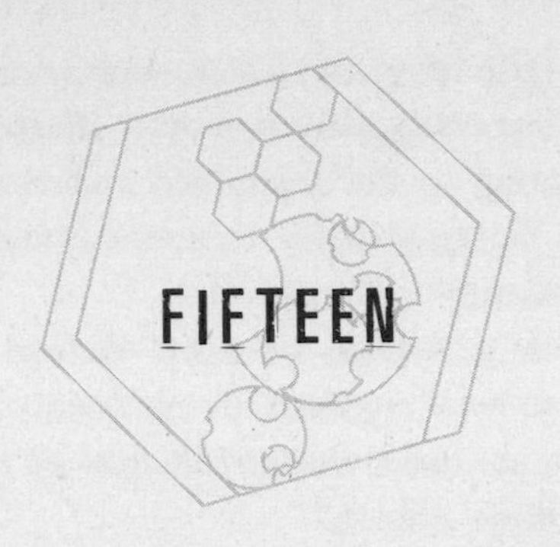

FIFTEEN

The noise died away and for several moments there was silence.

Defron struggled to his feet. 'What is the meaning of this?' he demanded. His voice was quavering as he addressed the two mirrored figures looking down at him. 'General Orlo? What is going on here?'

'Victory,' both Orlos said together.

'I don't understand.'

'Of course you don't, you snivelling wretch,' the original Orlo declared. He stepped down from the dais and hauled Defron up until the man was on tip-toe, almost at eye level with the massive creature.

'You want to negotiate the red-line clauses?' Defron asked, his voice rising an octave.

'We will negotiate nothing. This fiasco ends now. I hold Castle Extremis, and my troops will crush any resistance.' Orlo let go of Defron, who sprawled on the floor at his feet. 'Negotiation is over.' He swept his arm across, pointing to the assembled audience. 'You will report that Zerugma holds Extremis through right of conquest and might of arms.'

'This castle is neutral territory,' Defron thundered. He seemed to have regained his confidence as he stood up again. 'It is under the jurisdiction of the Galactic Alliance. Colonel Blench!'

Blench was at the back of the Great Hall. Martha saw he had been watching events impassively. Now the Colonel stepped into the aisle. 'Sir,' he acknowledged.

'You will please relieve the Zerugian troops of their illegal weapons and escort the General – the Generals,' Defron corrected himself, 'to the negotiating chamber. We will sort this out in private.'

'And what do you suggest, High Minister Defron, sir, if General Orlo doesn't agree?' Blench asked calmly.

Orlo laughed, his reflection mirroring him. 'I most certainly do not agree.'

More of the GA soldiers were arriving at the back of the hall. They deployed along the side and down the aisle in professional, practised moves. Their weapons trained on the dais.

'Could I say something, before anyone does anything a bit, well, *silly*?' The Doctor was walking slowly up the aisle, hands deep in his pockets. 'Won't take long, promise.'

Behind Orlo and his reflected self, the Zerugian

soldiers had spread out across the dais and to the side of the hall.

'What is it, Doctor?' Orlo's reflection demanded.

The Doctor stopped in front of the dais. He leaned forward slightly as if to get a better view of his own reflection in the mirror. He licked the ends of his fingers and slicked down his hair. 'Surrender,' he said.

'What?'

'Surrender. You're outnumbered and outgunned. Defron is right, this isn't the way. You want glory and honour for your people? Then fight for it at the negotiating table. That's the way wars are won and victory is achieved – victory for everyone. This way, your way, everyone loses. So do the right thing. Be brave. You have one chance – surrender.'

'Outgunned?' Orlo, the real Orlo, laughed.

The Doctor shook his head in exasperation. 'Is that the only word you listened to? Didn't you hear any of the other things I said? But yes, if that's the only argument you'll understand, surrender because you will *lose*.'

For an answer, Orlo raised a hand. He snapped his clawed fingers together. Immediately, the Zerugian soldiers arranged behind him levelled their weapons.

'You forget, Doctor, my troops are armed.'

'Really.'

'With guns that *work*.'

The Doctor seemed to freeze. 'Ah.' Then he smiled. 'Maybe I don't need guns.'

Blench was standing close behind the Doctor now.

'Give us the release codes,' he said. 'As a special agent and representative of the Galactic Alliance, you can authorise use of weapons. Give us the codes now – our guns won't work without the codes.'

The Doctor was still staring at the two generals, indistinguishable except that they wore their eyepatches on different sides. 'Is that what you want?' the Doctor asked. 'I give Blench and his men the codes and you all shoot it out? I tell you, Orlo, it's over. Surrender now, lay down your guns and we can still negotiate. But if I have to give the release codes then that means weapons will be released for use. And if that happens it's tantamount to a declaration of war. Zerugma against the Galactic Alliance – that's not the way to win anything.'

At the back of the hall, Martha held her breath. Of course the Doctor didn't have any codes to give. The GA troops really were powerless. But would Orlo take the risk? She breathed a heavy sigh of relief as Orlo said:

'Very well, Doctor.' The two Generals turned to look at each other. Then the real Orlo went on: 'Give Colonel Blench the release codes.'

The Doctor's mouth dropped open. 'What?' He leaned forward. 'What?' He shook his head. 'What?!'

'Or could it be,' Orlo's reflection said quietly, 'that you don't know the codes?'

'Doctor!' Blench said urgently.

'I'll tell him,' the Doctor warned.

The two massive reptiles in front of him folded their arms. There was muttering from the audience. Several people slipped out the back of the room, but most were torn between fear and the chance of reporting on a huge news story.

'You're no more a GA representative than I am,' Orlo said, his voice picked up and amplified by the microphone he wore. 'I have friends at Galactic Central, and they tell me no observers were dispatched to these talks. It was felt that the pressure of observation might endanger the chances of agreement.'

'Doctor?' Blench said.

'Tell him he's wrong,' Defron insisted. 'The point about covert observers is that no one knows about them. I only know because the GA Council themselves told me they have an agent here. Two agents, in fact. The Doctor and Miss Martha.'

'Ah,' the Doctor said. 'Well, that's not strictly true, is it? I mean, they didn't actually give you our names, did they?'

'Well no,' Defron admitted. 'But who else could it be?'

'No one,' Orlo said. He sounded bored. 'I told you, no agents or observers were despatched. So I suggest you tell your men to drop their weapons, Colonel Blench. I suggest *you* surrender.'

The Doctor held up his hand. 'You really don't get it, do you?' No agents were despatched because the GA agents were already here.'

Orlo stepped to the front of the dais and leaned towards the Doctor, towering over him. 'You are bluffing.'

'Want to bet on it? And I'll tell you another thing: your army there isn't as mighty and all-powerful as you think. Because the Mortal Mirror doesn't work in the way you believe it does. Thorodin – or whoever it was you had imitating him – he tried to tell you. But I don't think he ever got round to it.'

'Where is Sastrak?'

'Was that his name?'

'He is dead?' Orlo demanded.

'Shattered. And I mean that. Your army, even your reflection standing beside you there – they're all made of glass.'

'You lie!' General Orlo swung round to look at his troops. Then back to the Doctor. 'I don't believe you.'

The Doctor shrugged. 'Suit yourself. But when Blench gets his release codes, you'll soon find out. Last chance – surrender.'

'Never!' Orlo snarled. 'There are no codes. You think I haven't monitored and checked every transmission in and out of Extremis? No codes have been sent.'

'Really?'

'Yes.'

'You're sure?'

'Positive.'

'Maybe he's right, Doctor,' Blench said quietly.

'No, no, no,' the Doctor said. 'No, I won't have that. I mean, there are other ways the codes could have been sent here. Ways that weren't monitored. Aren't there?'

'You clutch at straws, Doctor,' Orlo said. 'It is time to

end this.' He raised his hand again.

'Surely the codes could have been sent by post, or courier, or carrier pigeon, or – well, somehow.'

The Doctor turned to the audience, most of whom were now ducking down behind the chairs and any other cover they could find.

'Could have been narrow-beamed directly to the agents,' Bill called from the back of the room.

'There you are then,' the Doctor said happily.

'Encrypted for the receiver only,' Bott agreed. 'That wouldn't go through main comms and no one else would detect it.'

'It would work a treat,' Bill told everyone. 'Wouldn't it, Bott?'

'Oh, it certainly would, Bill.'

General Orlo was shaking his massive scaly head. His reflected self mirrored the action. 'A narrow-beam direct communication has to go to a receiver. It can't be used to communicate with an agent. It's a network protocol for sending instructions and data to equipment and technology.'

'You mean, like a robot?' the Doctor asked.

Orlo blinked. A trail of viscous saliva dripped from his open jaw.

'I really don't think there's any option left,' the Doctor said sadly. 'Colonel Blench, the Galactic Alliance authorises you for use of weapons.'

'No!' Orlo roared.

'Then surrender!' the Doctor shouted at him.

In reply, Orlo ripped the microphone from his breastplate and dashed it to the floor.

And from the back of the hall, Bill said: 'The GA Release Code is nine seven four oblique-stroke two.'

'Colonel Blench, you have use of weapons,' Bott added. 'Doesn't he, Bill?'

'He certainly does, Bott,' Bill said. 'Take cover.'

From all round the hall there came the sound of the GA soldiers entering the release code into their weapons. The double-click of power-rounds loading into the guns as they were made ready to fire.

'You are outnumbered and outgunned,' Colonel Blench told General Orlo.

Orlo's lips curled back from his stained, yellowing teeth. 'You think so.' He stepped aside, his alter ego moving across the dais in the opposite direction. In the mirror behind, another group of Zerugian soldiers marched into the reflection of the Great Hall. Then another. And another. Marching towards the mirror, and stepping out of it into the real world.

There was chaos. Martha dived behind the sound desk where Bill and Bott were standing. Soldiers raced for cover. The press and dignitaries in the audience were under their chairs, hiding behind the huge speakers, or crawling, staggering, running for the doors. The Zerugians already in the hall advanced, while more and more emerged from the rippling surface of the Mortal Mirror.

Colonel Blench was shouting to his troops to wait,

and to Orlo and the Zerugians to surrender.

But after a moment, his voice was lost in the deafening roar of the guns.

The Doctor dived under the side table with the treaty book on it.

'You all right?' he asked as he pulled his feet out of sight after him. It was a bit cramped, but it would have to do. And if he was going to end this madness he needed to talk to the person already hiding under the table and now sitting with her legs pulled up under her chin beside him.

'I hoped he'd surrender, once he saw that Colonel Blench had overwhelmingly more soldiers. But he didn't. Because he hasn't. Which is annoying.' The Doctor lifted the edge of the velvet table cloth to peer out.

The GA soldiers were retreating towards the main doors, forced back by the sheer numbers of Zerugians from the mirror.

'Where have they all come from?' the Doctor wondered out loud. 'He can't have hidden that many in there, unless...' He shook his head as he realised. 'Multiplied in the mirror. Reflections of reflections of reflections.'

A bullet hammered into a Zerugian close to the table. It caught the creature in the leg, shattering it. The Zerugian collapsed, one arm breaking as it hit the stone floor. The side of its head sheared off. But still it tried to drag itself on, firing its own weapon as it went.

'Brittle, but resilient,' the Doctor murmured. 'Determined. Obsessed, even. We need more than bullets. Bullets never solved anything. We need...' He turned towards the girl. '... You.'

Her eyes were wide. 'What can I do?'

The Doctor held up his sonic screwdriver. 'Get this to Martha. Tell her it's all set and ready to rock and roll. Bill and Bott will know how to use it.'

'And what's it do?'

Before the Doctor could answer, the cloth was pulled aside and a snarling green face appeared. A gun swung up to cover the Doctor and Janna. The snarl became a reptilian smile as a claw tightened on the trigger.

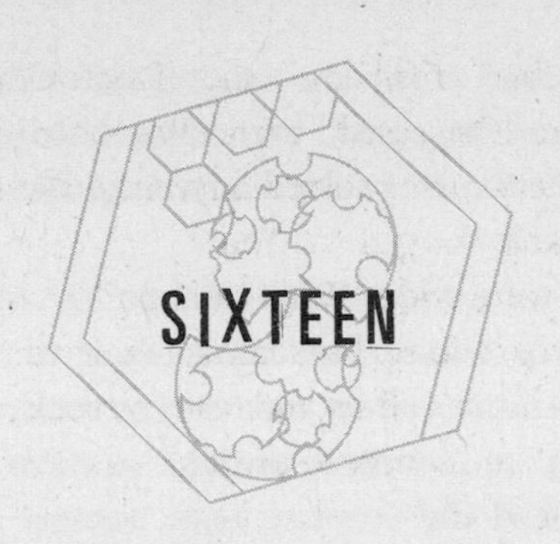

SIXTEEN

Janna shrieked as the grotesque, green face pulled back, a fine maze of cracks webbing across its scaled cheek.

The Doctor thrust the sonic screwdriver right at the Zerugian and switched it on. The Zerugian's face was illuminated by the bright blue light for a moment. A high-pitched squeal erupted from the sonic screwdriver. The mass of cracks became splits, widening and growing. Then the whole creature exploded in a shattering blast of glass fragments.

With his hands over his face, the Doctor dived across Janna to protect her from the flying shards.

'*That*'s what it does,' he said. 'But it's too focused to be much use except right up close like that.' He held out the sonic for her to take. 'Get it to Martha. I'll distract them all, make sure you're safe.'

Janna looked at the Doctor. Her eyes were still wide with fear, and he smiled and nodded to reassure her. After a moment, she nodded back and crawled out from under the table.

The Doctor jumped to his feet on the other side of the table. His hands were thrust deep in his pockets and his face set in a stern, uncompromising expression. Immediately a Zerugian turned towards him. The Doctor shoved the creature aside. Its feet skidded on broken glass and it crashed to the floor. The Doctor stepped over the shattered body.

'Orlo!' he shouted. 'You have to end this. You stop it, or I will. Your choice.'

There were two General Orlos, but he didn't care which one he spoke to. They would be of the same mind.

'And how can you stop me now?' a voice said from behind the Doctor.

He switched on a grin and spun round. The room was falling quiet. GA soldiers and Zerugian warriors holding their positions as they watched the Doctor and Orlo standing in the middle of the carnage – broken glass, shattered warriors, dead and dying soldiers…

The Doctor took a moment to look around before he answered. The other Orlo – the reflection, the Doctor saw from the side he wore his eyepatch – was halfway down the hall, leading his warriors against Colonel Blench's forces. Blench and his men had taken what cover they could. There was a barricade hastily built from piled-up chairs and behind that was the sound desk. The Doctor could see Martha with Bill and Bott, and he could see Janna crawling between the legs of the jungle-pile of chairs as she worked her way to the back of the hall.

'Oh, I'll stop you,' the Doctor said. 'You and your army of glass. Delicate stuff, glass.'

'I'm not made of glass,' Orlo said. 'And if I were, is that really any more fragile than human life? Than flesh and blood and bone and sinew?'

'That depends, doesn't it? Glass people may not bleed, but they can certainly break.' He drew circles in the glittering debris with the toe of his shoe. 'Ashes to ashes or sand to sand. Same difference in the end. And make no mistake, this *is* the end. Stop now. Surrender while you can.'

Orlo leaned forward, so close the Doctor could feel the cold breath on his face. 'Never.'

The Doctor wiped flecks of saliva from his face. 'I was afraid you'd say that. I'm sorry.' He raised his voice and called to the back of the Great Hall: 'Now, Martha!'

Janna ran past the soldiers at the makeshift barricade, holding out the sonic screwdriver.

'What's he want me to do with this?' Martha asked, taking it from the girl.

'It breaks glass. But it's too focused,' Janna said.

'Er – so?!'

Janna shook her head. 'He said you'd know what to do. You and Bill and Bott.'

Hearing his name, Bill turned from adjusting controls on the sound desk. 'That the sonic?' he asked.

'Looks like it could be a sonic to me,' Bott said.

'Good. Been waiting for that,' Bill said.

Martha handed the sonic screwdriver to Bill. His spindly metal fingers snapped closed on it and he passed it across to Bott.

'Reckon this'll do the trick, Bott?'

'I reckon it will, Bill.'

'In your own time,' the Doctor's voice called from the other side of the barricade.

'You are wasting my time and your life,' Orlo's snarling tones replied.

Bott took the sonic screwdriver and set about attaching it to a mass of wires and components erupting from the centre of the sound desk.

'Just link up the audio feed,' Bott said.

'And then we can start,' Bill added.

'Start what?' Martha asked.

Bill looked at Bott.

Bott looked at Bill.

'This!' they both said together.

'Don't lecture me about time,' the Doctor was saying. His words faded under the building hum of noise that emerged from the speakers along the side of the hall.

'Your time is over!' Even Orlo's vicious snarls were lost as the sound continued to build. It rose in volume and in pitch. Martha and Janna had their hands clamped over their ears.

There was a violent crash as part of the barricade collapsed. Martha thought at first it had been shaken apart by the sound waves, but a Zerugian staggered through the gap, hurling chairs aside as he came.

But he was shaking, his features a shimmering blur. He raised his hands to his head, staggering back and forth. He lurched in front of one of the massive speakers. Martha could see the grille across the front of the speaker rippling. And still the sound grew and rose.

Until the Zerugian exploded in a shower of glittering fragments of glass.

More Zerugians were following the first. But they too were staggering and vibrating. One fell forward as its leg shattered. Another crashed into the speaker and was blown back in a blizzard of fragments.

But still more were coming. The GA soldiers were painfully deafened. They weren't exploding like the glass Zerugians, but they were unable to fight back. Another Zerugian shattered to pieces in front of the barricade. Then another.

Only one Zerugian staggered on. The glass reflection of General Orlo, face cracked – a deep line running along his scar, but splitting the eyepatch as well. One of his arms ended in a jagged stump at the elbow. His armour – his body – was chipped and scratched and cracked.

But he lumbered towards the sound desk.

Martha staggered out to stop him, shoulder barging into the Zerugian, unable to take her hands from her ears. She could barely see now, her eyes were watering so much. But Orlo's reflection thrust her aside. He lunged over the sound desk.

'Stop him!' Martha yelled. 'He's going for the sonic!' But her cry was lost in the cacophony.

A glass claw clamped down on the mass of cables and the sonic screwdriver. Cracks rippled up the fingers and forearm. The whole of Orlo's body crazed with a spider's web of fractures.

Bott grabbed for Orlo's hand, trying to pull it away.

He was too late. Orlo wrenched the sonic clear, and hurled it away. The sound cut out. There was a snapping sound as the sonic hammered into the wall by the door. It fell to the floor in pieces.

For a moment there was complete and utter silence. More than half of Orlo's army lay in shattered ruins across the floor of the Great Hall. Many, though, were still standing, their bodies glazed and cracked. But intact.

Then the glass Orlo turned and reached for Janna, his broken claws raking down towards her face. Janna screamed from point-blank range.

The claws shattered. The hand exploded. Orlo's legs folded under him, collapsing under his own weight.

'That's it!' Martha gasped. 'Keep screaming – Janna keep screaming. And you two,' she yelled at Bill and Bott, 'put it through the speakers.'

With a final snarl of anger and pain, the glass Orlo lashed out. The remains of his shattered arm swept Janna off her feet. She fell sideways, head cracking into the side of the sound desk, as Orlo himself fell back in fragments to the floor.

Martha was at Janna's side in a moment. There was a cut on the girl's head, and her eyelids flickered.

'No, no, no,' Martha told her, cradling the girl in her arms. But Janna's head sagged and she was unconscious. Martha laid her down carefully on the floor. She would be all right, and there would be time to take care of her later – she hoped. But first it was up to her to stop the rest of the Zerugians.

'Microphone?' Bill offered.

Martha took it. And screamed.

She shouted and yelled and shrieked till she was hoarse.

But the Zerugians were forcing their way through the barricade, unaffected. The GA soldiers were falling back, helpless as they ran out of ammunition.

'It's the wrong pitch,' Bott said. He was working frantically at the controls. 'I can only amplify and boost the wave form.'

'Can't change the pitch,' Bill agreed. 'We need Janna. We need her screams.'

But the girl lay unconscious on the floor beside them as General Orlo's Zerugian army advanced through the Great Hall of Castle Extremis.

When Janna's scream cut out, the Doctor knew he had problems. He'd made good use of the distraction as the sonic sound wave cut down so many of Orlo's soldiers.

He had run to the Mortal Mirror and adjusted the controls so that it was just a mirror again. Luckily whoever had set it up – Thorodin probably – had not had time or been bothered to reset the deadlock seals. No more reflected Zerugians would be coming through.

But, even deprived of reinforcements, Orlo still had enough troops who had survived the carnage wrought by the sonic screwdriver to take Castle Extremis. Then he could let in reinforcements from Zerugma – real warriors who wouldn't shatter and break under a sonic assault.

General Orlo knew that. His lips were curling from his jagged teeth in a satisfied smile as he advanced on the Doctor.

'We could talk about this,' the Doctor said. 'I mean, if you want. That is, I'm up for it. What about you?'

Orlo's arm struck out and claws closed on the Doctor's neck.

'Or not,' the Doctor managed to gasp. 'I'm easy about it, actually. Tell you what – you decide.'

Then he was tumbling through the air and rolling across the dais and landing heavily on the stone floor. Strong hands – human hands – helped the Doctor to his feet and he dusted himself down.

'Thank you, Mr Stellman. But don't feel you have to hang on here for me.'

'I'm not,' Stellman said.

The Doctor could see Lady Casaubon sitting pale and weak on a chair at the side of the dais, out of the way of the ongoing battle. 'Ah,' he said. 'Yes, duty and loyalty and friendship often decide our choices.'

'I've made my choice, Doctor,' Stellman said.

As Orlo's hands grabbed the Doctor's shoulders from behind, Stellman opened his jacket – just enough for the Doctor to see the sparkle of glass, the flash of reflected light from the gun tucked into Stellman's inside pocket.

'You're finished, Doctor,' Orlo snarled. 'You can do nothing.'

'Maybe,' the Doctor said. 'But I've got something you haven't. Something that can still win the day and sort you out. Something I bet you've not even thought of.'

Orlo gave a derisive laugh. 'And what is that?'

'Friends. I've got Martha. She's brilliant, she is. She'll think of something.'

Some of the Zerugians were damaged – chipped and broken. All of them were weakened and cracked. But they were coming through the gaps in the barricade quicker than Colonel Blench and his depleted force could hold them off. With little or no ammunition, the fighting was hand to hand. Soldiers were hurling chairs, swinging their guns like swords, kicking and punching.

Bott had taken up guard position in front of the sound equipment. One of his heavy arms flailed and thumped. The other was fitted with a blowtorch attachment – the jet of intense blue flame melting into a Zerugian that hurled itself at him. His other arm punched the blackened, twisted remains to pieces.

Martha was kneeling beside Janna, gently patting the girl's cheeks. But there was no sign of her coming round.

'Let me,' a voice said. A figure crouched down and lifted the girl. It was Gonfer. 'Let me get her away from here.'

Martha bit her lip – without Janna, they were lost. But she couldn't keep the child here. She nodded.

Gonfer lifted Janna in his arms. His face was streaked with tears. 'I told her not to – I said there must be another way. But she wouldn't listen. It's my fault, and she's going to die again – because of me.'

'She'll be all right,' Martha insisted above the shouts and the shots and the crash of breaking glass. 'Get Janna away from here, take her to one of her hiding places. You'll both be all right.'

'Not Janna,' Gonfer said, his voice catching in his throat. 'Tylda.'

Then the screaming started.

The sound was deafening. The girl's screams echoed round the hall, accompanied by the percussion of exploding glass.

Only the Mortal Mirror seemed immune as Orlo's troops – already cracked and weakened by the sound wave generated by the sonic screwdriver – shattered to fragments around him.

Orlo held the Doctor by the shoulders and watched in horrified amazement.

'I did tell you,' the Doctor said. 'Didn't I?' he said to Stellman. 'Tell him I told him.'

With a furious roar, Orlo hurled the Doctor aside. 'You're nobody,' he hissed. 'You are not even fit to be a hostage.'

'Well, excuse me, I'm the guy who sorted out your crack troops.' The Doctor's hand flew to his mouth. 'Sorry, a bit tactless there. Maybe "crack" wasn't the best word.' He ducked to allow a shower of glass to fly past.

But Orlo wasn't listening. He leaped forward and dragged Lady Casaubon up from her chair.

'I'm getting out of here, Doctor,' he said. 'Or she dies.'

The girl's mouth was wide open as she screamed. A network of cracks spread across her face, along her arms, over her whole body. Martha could only watch, horrified.

Bill and Bott were frantically rewiring the damaged part of the sound desk where Orlo had ripped the wires out.

'We can't record her till it's mended,' Bill was saying.

'Can't play back the recording we can't make either,' Bott agreed.

'Stop!' another voice shouted.

The cloaked figure of a monk staggered through the doors. 'Enough!' Manfred Grieg croaked through cracked glass lips.

Tylda stopped screaming. Her body creaked as she turned to face Grieg. She shivered, but remained intact.

'Is it over?' she asked.

Grieg's face was also cracked and crazed. 'It's over,' he said.

'You did it,' Martha said, struggling to hold back her emotions. 'You saved us all.'

The girl was holding up her hand, staring at the lines and fissures where the glass had fractured inside. 'I did it,' she said quietly. 'Will Tylda be all right?'

The claws were pressed into the wrinkled skin of Lady Casaubon's neck.

'If you try to stop me, I will kill her,' Orlo hissed. 'A moment is all it takes.'

His feet crunched on broken glass as he dragged the woman across the hall.

The Doctor stood impassive. 'Where do you think you can go? What can you do?'

'I can assemble another army, and this time we *will* take Castle Extremis.'

Lady Casaubon struggled to shake her head. 'No, Orlo – haven't you learned anything? Haven't you lost anyone?'

'Silence, hag!' Orlo roared.

With a whimper, Lady Casaubon sagged. Orlo bent with her as she became a dead weight. Her arms trailed along the floor for a moment before Orlo hauled her upright again.

'Let me go – please,' Lady Casaubon said.

'Never. You are weak and decrepit, just as your people

are weak and decrepit. You will never win against Zerugian might.'

Lady Casaubon sighed. She looked at the Doctor, and at Stellman standing powerless next to him. 'What can you do?' she said, like a teacher talking about an unruly child. 'This is your fault, you fool,' she added. She was speaking to Orlo, turning, bringing up her small, ancient hand. And stabbing the long icicle of glass she had scooped from the floor into the back of Orlo's claw.

The General's hand spasmed and he let go of Lady Casaubon as he cried out in surprise and pain. He wrenched out the glass and reached for her again, his eyes blazing with fury.

He never reached her. A glass bullet hammered into his skull, and General Orlo crashed to the floor, lying dead in the remains of his splintered army.

'Thank you, Stellman,' Lady Casaubon said calmly. 'Perhaps now they will send us someone who can negotiate the Zerugian position sensibly.' She turned to the Doctor. 'And thank you,' she said. 'We owe you everything. We owe you our future.'

The Doctor nodded. He looked round the Great Hall, and saw Martha walking slowly towards him. 'I won't say it's been a pleasure,' he said quietly.

But his words were lost in the noise from the speakers all around as Bill's electronic tones exclaimed: 'And just who do you think they'll expect to clear all this up, Bott?'

SEVENTEEN

Most of the glass had been swept up – despite the complaints from Bill and Bott that this was above and beyond the call of duty and that, as accredited GA agents now out in the open, they ought to be exempt from any further cleaning duties.

As the two robots grumbled on in the background, the Doctor and Martha stood in front of the Mortal Mirror.

'How come it didn't break?' Martha asked.

'Because it is not made of real glass,' Manfred Grieg told her. He was still wearing the monk's outfit he had taken from Gonfer. With the hood pushed back, he looked like a cracked, chipped statue.

'It isn't a real mirror at all,' the Doctor agreed. 'Otherwise we'd be on the lookout for a girl with a red balloon,' he added quietly, before going on: 'There's a whole world in there. It gets darker the further into it you get. But you know we're going to have to shut it off permanently, close the doorway between the worlds.'

'I know,' Grieg said. 'You can rely on us to keep it closed. Just as I have these past long years.'

'Us?' Martha said.

At that moment, Defron came hurrying across the Great Hall. 'Oh, Doctor, and Martha, I'm so glad I caught you. Gonfer said you were preparing to leave.'

'Our work here is done,' the Doctor told him. 'You know how it is – places to see, people to go, worlds to save, lives to change. Sort of thing.'

'But the GA will want to thank you. The General Secretary herself is coming, along with the new Zerugian representative who apparently is very keen to get the treaty signed. It seems that General Orlo was something of a rogue element.'

'Rogue, certainly,' Martha said.

'And since you know Madame Secretary…' Defron went on.

'Do you?' Martha said to the Doctor, surprised.

'Oh yes, great friends. We're like…' The Doctor struggled to cross his fingers, gave up and held them apart in a victory V instead. 'Like that. Tell you what,' he went on quickly to Defron, 'we'll stay if we can, but no promises. We have so much to do. I have to mend my sonic screwdriver, for one thing.'

Defron nodded enthusiastically. 'That is so good of you, Doctor.'

'But whatever happens,' the Doctor said, taking Defron by the arm and leading his aside, 'don't get too chummy with her. If you want my advice, you'll pal up with Teddy Enkit. Maybe put a small bet on him being GA General Secretary within the year.'

Defron was surprised. 'You think so? But he's so inexperienced.'

'Rising star. Trust me.' The Doctor winked and steered Defron towards the door.

'What was that all about?' Martha asked when he returned.

'I really shouldn't be giving clues,' the Doctor said. 'But Defron will be the main sponsor and proposer of Edward Enkit for the role of General Secretary when Canasta Ventron is taken ill next year. Good chap, Teddy.'

'You should put that in your diary,' Martha told Grieg.

He chuckled. 'My diary is finished. It has served its purpose.' He took the glass book from a pocket of his cloak. It looked less fragile and dusty than when the Doctor and Martha had found it hidden in the wall.

'So why did you write it all down anyway?' Martha wondered. 'Why not just tell us what was going on?'

Grieg handed the diary to the Doctor. 'I think you should have this. It isn't quite up to date, but I have seen that it will serve its purpose.'

'Thank you,' the Doctor said, taking the delicate glass book.

Grieg turned to Martha. 'Who would listen to the ramblings of an old man?' he asked. 'Tales of a world behind the mirror, of reptile creatures and galactic wars, of treaties and murders and politics and trickery? No.' He shook his head, the light reflecting off the broken edges of his nose and the cracks in his cheek. 'But write them down, makes these things into a story, and perhaps – just perhaps – someone will want to know what happens.'

'Must you go back inside the mirror?' Martha asked.

'This is no longer my world. There is no place for me here. And it is still a trap. If I miss my footing, if I knock against a table or brush against the wall, I could fracture and die.' He held up his hand, as he had before, and it seemed to Martha that it was even more cracked and fragile than it had been the first time. 'I would not last long in your world, and the pain – every day the pain would increase, until…' He lowered his arm and turned away.

Martha followed the old man's gaze and saw that Janna and Gonfer had come into the hall. With them was another girl – the image of Janna, but her face, even her clothes, were a web-work of lines and cracks.

'He's going to lose her again, or so he thinks,' the Doctor said as the three figures approached.

'You mean Janna?' Martha said. 'Or is it Tylda?'

'Well, that's the problem, isn't it? No one could tell them apart, not by looking at them.' The Doctor sighed. 'One of them nice, the other not so pleasant. She wound him up something rotten, and he chased her into the garden. He thought he was chasing Tylda and it was really Janna – that's why she was so scared. He was chasing the wrong girl.'

'The kitchen boy?' Martha said.

'Gonfer. He worked in the kitchens then. He went after Tylda, but he found Janna and didn't realise. It was Janna who died out there in the garden. Gonfer can never forgive himself. That's why he looks after Tylda now – though he did think it was Janna. Till he realised the truth.'

'But, why didn't she tell him?'

'Because it was her fault too. She teased and taunted him, and drove him to do it. She thought it was fun to upset him, and her sister died for it. And now,' the Doctor said quietly, 'they're going to lose her all over again.'

Gonfer looked pale and tired. Janna – or rather, Tylda – had a bruise on her forehead. Her cheeks were stained with tears.

The glass girl walked slowly and carefully, watching where she put every tentative footstep.

'Please stay,' Tylda said, almost in tears. 'Please, I can't lose you again.'

'I *am* you. I'm not our sister,' the glass girl said, and her own voice was cracked with emotion. 'And I can't stay. If I do...' She turned away.

Grieg took a step towards her. 'She is right. Our place is in the mirror. Look at her – so fragile, so delicate. She is lucky to have survived all this.' He opened his hands and turned to indicate the whole room. 'Would you have her stay? To stay is certain pain and then death for her. Even more certain than it is for me, and I too must go.'

'Can't you do anything?' Gonfer asked the Doctor.

He shook his head. 'It's too late, I'm afraid.'

'But she'll be safe in the mirror world,' Martha said.

'Everything has its own time and space,' the Doctor agreed. 'Hers is in there. And ours... well, ours is in a sort of box, actually. And we should be on our way too.' He pulled Gonfer into a hug. 'Come on, big fellah – you'll be OK. Look after Tylda.'

'I will.' Gonfer's lips were tight as he pulled away, as he held back his emotion.

'And you look after Gonfer,' the Doctor told Tylda, hugging her tight.

She hugged him back. 'I will,' she promised. 'He's my best friend.'

The girl was trembling as Martha hugged her. She shook hands with Gonfer, not sure how he'd cope with anything more.

The Doctor turned to Grieg. 'You'd best be going. Thanks for this.' He held up the diary.

'You know what to do with it, time traveller?' Grieg asked.

'Oh I think I can work it out.'

'That's another thing,' Martha said. 'How did you know we're time travellers?'

Gonfer's mouth was open in astonishment.

The Doctor grinned. 'Not hard to work out, really,' he said. 'When you think about it.'

'Goodbye, Doctor,' Grieg said. 'And thank you.'

'Thank *you*,' the Doctor countered. 'I won't shake your hand,' he said with a smile. 'Or yours,' he told the glass girl standing beside Grieg. 'You're so brave. Be strong. And look after the old gentleman.'

The girl nodded. 'Goodbye,' she said quietly. 'To all of you, goodbye.'

'Don't go!' Tylda sobbed. 'You can't go – please don't leave me.' She ran forward.

'Careful!' Martha warned as the two girls stood facing each other. Tylda had her arms open. Her reflection stood silent and still.

Then gently, so gently, Tylda closed her arms round the glass girl, barely touching her in the closest they could ever come to an embrace.

Moments later they stood looking at the Mortal Mirror. Tylda, Gonfer, the Doctor and Martha stared into the reflection of the Great Hall. A reflection that was not a reflection, where an old man made of glass and a delicate, brittle girl stared out at them. The girl placed her hand against the glass, and Tylda put her own hand over it.

They stood without moving, without speaking, tears rolling down their cheeks.

Then the mirror rippled and shimmered, and Tylda was sobbing at her reflection. Her mirror image. Her twin.

EIGHTEEN

A strange rasping, grating sound echoed through the corridors and passageways of Castle Extremis.

On the other side of the castle, a banquet was just beginning. Kendal Pennard, Lord High Advocate for Anthium and the Governor of Castle Extremis, was about to make a presentation to the man who had masterminded the recapture of Extremis after the Second Zerugian occupation. He was about to give him a mirror.

The two robots that were working in one of the conference rooms close to the main courtyard knew this. They had hung the mirror in the Great Hall – just as a hundred years later they would hang what they were told was its replica in the same place. But now they were getting on with more mundane tasks. It was their job to repair or replace the fabric and structure of the castle as it grew old and wore out, or was damaged in battle. They were repairing a wall.

'This stone's had it, Bott,' Bill said, jabbing at the wall with his metal arm. A spray of pale dust erupted from the metal point.

'Better replace it then, Bill,' Bott said. 'Give me the measurements and I'll cut one to fit, then we can chop this one out.'

The tall, slim man standing in the doorway watched with interest as the robots went about their task.

'You know,' he announced as Bott lifted the crumbling stone out of the wall, 'you're very good at this.'

'Had a lot of practice,' Bott told him.

'Best in the business,' Bill said.

'And who might you be?' Bott asked.

'Not time and motion come to check up on us?' Bill said.

'Not time and motion, no. Well...' The man stuffed his hands in his coat pockets and walked across to inspect the hole they had made in the wall. 'Not motion, anyway.'

'So – can we do something for you?' Bill enquired.

'Or are you just going to stand around and get in the way?' Bott asked.

'Sorry.' The man stepped back and gestured for them to carry on.

Bott lifted the stone he had just cut and lined it up with the hole. Bill steadied the heavy load as Bott inched it forwards.

The man cleared his throat.

Bill and Bott stopped. The stone remained motionless.

'Problem?' Bill asked.

'Something you'd like to say?' Bott checked.

'No, no. It's looking good,' the man said. 'Excellent in fact. Brilliant. I was just wondering though…'

'Yes?' Bott said.

'What?' Bill asked.

The man was holding something. Something he had taken from his pocket. It was rectangular, and looked like it was made of translucent plastic or glass. 'I was wondering if I could pop this behind the stone?'

'Why?' Bill asked.

'What for?' Bott wanted to know.

'Well, actually it's to impress a friend of mine. A young lady,' the man confided. 'Then I'll come back later, and find it again. As if by magic.'

'Behind our stone,' Bill said.

'This stone we're about to put in,' Bott added.

'That very one,' the man agreed.

'How will you get it out again?' Bott asked. 'We're not having you messing up our work you know.'

'This is serious stuff,' Bill said. 'Not some parlour trick. This stone'll be in place till it crumbles away and needs replacing again.'

'And that won't be for a hundred years, give or take.'

'With the slow decay you get from the osmotic rendition caused by the barrier.'

'So, I'll need to come back in a hundred years?' the man said.

'Afraid so,' Bott told him.

'Near enough,' Bill agreed.

'Right. OK. Fair enough.' The man beamed at them. 'I'll do that then.'

Bill and Bott looked at each other. Then they looked at the man, who was still grinning at them with satisfaction.

'Sure?' Bill asked.

'Absolutely.'

'Positive?' Bott checked.

'Hundred per cent.'

'Is that glass?' Bill asked.

'Sort of,' the man told them.

'It'll scratch,' Bott told him.

'Wrap it in a bit of cloth,' Bill suggested. 'There's some down there by the cutting tools.'

The man wrapped a piece of cloth round the glass box or whatever it was. Then he pushed it carefully to the back of the hole Bill and Bott had cut in the wall. He stepped back to allow them to fit the new piece of stone. When they'd finished, the hole was closed, hiding the small bundle of cloth.

'Thanks.'

'No problem.'

'Don't mention it.'

'See you in a hundred years.' The man paused in the doorway. 'Oh, and if you could make like you've never seen me before, that'd be a big help.'

'With impressing the young lady?' Bill said.

'Amongst other things. I'm cheating a bit by being here really. Tell you what,' he said as a thought occurred to him. 'Don't sneak on me, and I'll put in a word for you with the Galactic Alliance.'

'You're with the Galactic Alliance?' Bill was impressed.

'Didn't think they operated in this sector,' Bott said.

'All a bit hush-hush,' the man told them. 'But we're always on the lookout for reliable agents.'

'What do we need to do?' Bill asked.

'You can rely on us,' Bott assured him.

'I know,' the man said. 'Someone will be in touch. And they will give you a special code, though they won't expect you ever to need it.'

'Sounds like work for work's sake,' Bott grumbled.

'And we know all about *that*,' Bill said.

'You will need it though,' the man went on. 'It'll be important, really important. And when I ask you for it, I want to hear that release code loud and clear, understand?'

'Yes, sir,' Bill and Bott said together.

'Er,' Bill said, 'release code for what?'

But the man had gone.

Moments later, a breeze blew the dust across the floor as Bill and Bott worked on the next section of wall that needed repairing. If there was a strange sound accompanying it, a sound like reality itself splitting open, then Bott's drill was making so much noise they didn't notice.

A hundred years later – give or take, more or less – a little girl in a hidden room concealed behind the wall of a castle corridor slipped into a restless sleep.

A looking glass hung on the wall opposite the bed. Reflected in it, another girl slept restlessly, mirroring the real girl. Both turned together, breathed together, and finally woke up together.

Both girls pushed back their blankets and walked towards the mirror. Each raised a hand and pressed it to the glass, just for a moment.

'I miss you,' the little girl said.

'I know,' her reflection answered. 'I miss you too.'

'You'll always be there, won't you?'

'Always. I'm the girl in the mirror.'

The girls went back to their beds and were soon sleeping again. In the morning, perhaps, they would remember the brief waking in the night.

Or perhaps, after all, it was just a dream.

Acknowledgements

As ever, I am indebted to many people for their help and encouragement. Especially to Stephen Cole for his dependable and excellent structural editing, Gary Russell for keeping me honest and focused, and Steve Tribe for keeping me consistent and on schedule. Also, everyone at BBC Books for their unerring support and enthusiasm, especially Albert, Caroline, Nick and Mathew.

And, of course, huge thanks to Russell T Davies and the *Doctor Who* writers and production team for providing such wonderful toys for me to play with.

Also available from BBC Books
featuring the Doctor and Rose
as played by Christopher Eccleston and Billie Piper:

THE CLOCKWISE MAN
by Justin Richards

THE MONSTERS INSIDE
by Stephen Cole

WINNER TAKES ALL
by Jacqueline Rayner

THE DEVIANT STRAIN
by Justin Richards

ONLY HUMAN
by Gareth Roberts

THE STEALERS OF DREAMS
by Steve Lyons

Also available from BBC Books featuring the Doctor and Rose as played by David Tennant and Billie Piper:

THE STONE ROSE
by Jacqueline Rayner

THE FEAST OF THE DROWNED
by Stephen Cole

THE RESURRECTION CASKET
by Justin Richards

THE NIGHTMARE OF BLACK ISLAND
by Mike Tucker

THE ART OF DESTRUCTION
by Stephen Cole

THE PRICE OF PARADISE
by Colin Brake

Also available from BBC Books featuring the Doctor and Martha as played by David Tennant and Freema Agyeman:

STING OF THE ZYGONS
by Stephen Cole

THE LAST DODO
by Jacqueline Rayner

WOODEN HEART
by Martin Day

FOREVER AUTUMN
by Mark Morris

SICK BUILDING
by Paul Magrs

WETWORLD
by Mark Michalowski

Also available from BBC Books featuring the Doctor and Martha as played by David Tennant and Freema Agyeman:

Wishing Well

by Trevor Baxendale

ISBN 978 1 84607 348 9

UK £6.99 US $11.99/$14.99 CDN

The old village well is just a curiosity – something to attract tourists intrigued by stories of lost treasure, or visitors just making a wish. Unless something alien and terrifying could be lurking inside the well? Something utterly monstrous that causes nothing but death and destruction?

But who knows the real truth about the well? Who wishes to unleash the hideous force it contains? What terrible consequences will follow the search for a legendary treasure hidden at the bottom?

No one wants to believe the Doctor's warnings about the deadly horror lying in wait – but soon they'll wish they had...

Also available from BBC Books
featuring the Doctor and Martha
as played by David Tennant and Freema Agyeman:

The Pirate Loop

by Simon Guerrier

ISBN 978 1 84607 347 2
UK £6.99 US $11.99/$14.99 CDN

The Doctor's been everywhere and everywhen in the whole of the universe and seems to know all the answers. But ask him what happened to the Starship *Brilliant* and he hasn't the first idea. Did it fall into a sun or black hole? Was it shot down in the first moments of the galactic war? And what's this about a secret experimental drive?

The Doctor is skittish. But if Martha is so keen to find out he'll land the TARDIS on the *Brilliant,* a few days before it vanishes. Then they can see for themselves…

Soon the Doctor learns the awful truth. And Martha learns that you need to be careful what you wish for. She certainly wasn't hoping for mayhem, death, and badger-faced space pirates.

Also available from BBC Books featuring the Doctor and Martha as played by David Tennant and Freema Agyeman:

Peacemaker

by James Swallow

ISBN 978 1 84607 349 6

UK £6.99 US $11.99/$14.99 CDN

The peace and quiet of a remote homestead in the 1880s American West is shattered by the arrival of two shadowy outriders searching for 'the healer'. When the farmer refuses to help them, they raze the house to the ground using guns that shoot bolts of energy instead of bullets...

In the town of Redwater, the Doctor and Martha learn of a snake-oil salesman whose patent medicines actually cure his patient. But when the Doctor and Martha investigate they discover the truth is stranger, and far more dangerous.

Caught between the law of the gun and the deadly plans of intergalactic mercenaries, the Doctor and Martha are about to discover just how wild the West can become...

Also available from BBC Books featuring the Doctor and Martha as played by David Tennant and Freema Agyeman:

SnowGlobe 7

by Mike Tucker

ISBN 978 1 84607 421 9
UK £6.99 US $11.99/$14.99 CDN

Earth, 2099. Global warming is devastating the climate. The polar ice caps are melting.

In a desperate attempt at preservation, the governments of the world have removed vast sections of the Arctic and Antarctic and set them inside huge domes across the world. The Doctor and Martha arrive in SnowGlobe 7 in the Middle East, hoping for peace and relaxation. But they soon discover that it's not only ice and snow that has been preserved beneath the Dome.

While Martha struggles to help with an infection sweeping through the Dome, the Doctor discovers an alien threat that has lain hidden since the last ice age. A threat that is starting to thaw.

Also available from BBC Books featuring the Doctor and Martha as played by David Tennant and Freema Agyeman:

The Many Hands

by Dale Smith

ISBN 978 1 84607 422 6
UK £6.99 US $11.99/$14.99 CDN

The Nor' Loch is being filled in. If you ask the soldiers there, they'll tell you it's a stinking cesspool that the city can do without. But that doesn't explain why the workers won't go near the place without an armed guard.

That doesn't explain why they whisper stories about the loch giving up its dead, about the minister who walked into his church twelve years after he died...

It doesn't explain why, as they work, they whisper about a man called the Doctor.

And about the many hands of Alexander Monro.

Coming soon from BBC Books:

DOCTOR · WHO

Starships and Spacestations

by Justin Richards

ISBN 978 1 84607 423 3
£7.99 US $12.99/$15.99 CDN

The Doctor has his TARDIS to get him from place to place and time to time, but the rest of the Universe relies on more conventional transport... From the British Space Programme of the late twentieth century to Earth's Empire in the far future, from the terrifying Dalek Fleet to deadly Cyber Ships, this book documents the many starships and spacestations that the Doctor and his companions have encountered on their travels.

He has been held prisoner in space, escaped from the moon, witnessed the arrival of the Sycorax and the crash landing of a space pig... More than anyone else, the Doctor has seen the development of space travel between countless worlds.

This stunningly illustrated book tells the amazing story of Earth's ventures into space, examines the many alien fleets who have paid Earth a visit, and explores the other starships and spacestations that the Doctor has encountered on his many travels...